Gill Jacobs

D0525580

Escape from Danger

© Day One Publications 2013

First printed 2013

ISBN 978-1-84625-371-3

All Scripture quotations are from the **New International Version** 1984
Copyright © 1973, 1978, 1984

Published by Day One Publications
Ryelands Road, Leominster, HR6 8NZ

TEL 01568 613 740 FAX 01568 611 473

email—sales@dayone.co.uk

UK web site—www.dayone.co.uk

USA web site—www.dayonebookstore.com

Designed by **documen**
Printed by Orchard Press Cheltenham Ltd

Dedication

This book is dedicated to my husband John.

Chapter one

What was that? Naomi stopped dead in her tracks as a sudden sound broke the silence. She raised her hand to her mouth to stifle a scream. Had someone discovered her plan? Surely anyone would be able to hear the sound of her heart pounding in her chest. She strained her eyes in the darkness, trying to see what had caused the noise. Then she caught her breath as a large rat ran from the kitchen area, almost bumping into her as it passed, and scuttled off into the night.

Naomi waited until she was sure that the family was still sleeping. The frantic beating of her heart began to slow down, and her legs were trembling less now. She stretched out her hand and felt around for her mother's leather purse. Yes, there it was, hidden at the back of the cupboard. Quickly, Naomi dropped the purse into her bag, put two fresh loaves in on top, crept towards the back door and slipped out into the darkness.

Once outside she breathed more easily, but she wouldn't be safe until she had passed through the city gate and was on the road leading away from Damascus. Across the road was a checkpoint where a Roman soldier sat, but he was fast asleep and didn't stir as Naomi passed him. A little further on, she turned into Straight Street and was soon able to see the large gate in the city wall.

She knew the gate would be closed to keep out enemies who might try to steal into the city at night, but she also knew that very soon a crowd of people would gather here, ready to leave the city as soon as dawn came. Then the nightwatchman would open the gate and she would be able to mix with the crowds and escape. Softly, Naomi moved into the shadow of the wall, where the nightwatchman couldn't see her, and waited.

The plan had been worked out very carefully. It had taken Naomi three months to plan and to gather everything together. She had been very careful not to raise suspicion as she collected and hid what she would need, ready for today. In her bag was enough food for the long journey ahead—bread, dried olives, figs and dates—as well as a water flask, a blanket, a second pair of shoes, and her mother's purse. Naomi felt rather ashamed as she remembered how hard her mother had worked to be able to save the money in that purse. She had collected it coin by coin and hidden the purse away from the eyes of Naomi's stepfather, to prevent him finding it and spending it on one of his drinking bouts. From time to time her mother would use the precious money to buy extra milk and eggs for her children. 'But,' the girl told herself, 'I need the money more than Mother now.'

Naomi remembered very distinctly the moment she had decided she would leave home. It was the first time that her stepfather had beaten her with his stick. She could still see his angry face and hear his harsh words as he brought the stick down across her back. How she hated him! But his cruelty wasn't the main reason she had decided to leave. No. It had been the sight of her mother,

standing in the doorway clutching her new baby boy and
doing nothing to prevent Naomi from being beaten. Then
Naomi realized that she was unwanted, and she knew she
had to leave.

At first, she thought she would leave the city through
a hole in the city wall. She had searched and found a
place where even quite a large person could get through.
Often she returned to the wall to work out how she would
get down the other side. Unfortunately, there was such
a long drop to the ground below that Naomi had had to
give up that idea. No, she would have to find a time when
she could slip out through the city gate along with other
people. And today was that time.

From her hiding place, Naomi watched as people
started to gather at the gate, chattering and laughing
together, looking forward to the journey ahead. Now and
then, she recognized people she knew. When she saw her
best friend Miriam with her older brother Jacob and their
parents, she shrank back further into the shadows. It
would never do for them to see her.

Many people had a donkey or two with them to help
carry their belongings, and some of the better-off families
had camels laden with food, water and blankets. For them,
the journey would be easier. The youngest children would
be allowed to ride on the donkeys when they got tired, just
as Naomi had done in the past when she had travelled
with her mother and father. As she watched the happy
children with their parents, Naomi felt tears pricking her
eyes and she angrily rubbed them away with her hand.
This was no time for weakness. She was eleven years

old and almost grown up, and she didn't need family or friends.

As the sun slowly rose in the sky, more and more people gathered, until the whole area in front of the city entrance was crowded with people and the buzz of conversation had risen to a crescendo. The Jewish community was quite large in Damascus and all those who were able to travel were there. All, that is, apart from her family. Her mother had only just had her new baby and couldn't travel, and her stepfather had no interest in religious festivals.

Every now and then, Naomi looked anxiously up the road towards her home. Normally, her family would be asleep for at least another hour, but perhaps the sound of the travellers on the road outside would waken them and they might come looking for her. If her stepfather caught her, she knew she would be in for another beating.

With relief, Naomi saw the nightwatchman walking slowly towards the big gate and she watched impatiently as he swung it open and the people began to move together towards it. As they surged past her, she silently slipped from her hiding place and moved in among them so that she was carried along with the caravan of people and animals, out of the gate and onto the newly built Roman road that would take her away from Damascus.

She was free!

Chapter two

'Naomi! Is that you?' Naomi jumped as she heard the voice and turned to see the girl beside her. 'What are you doing here?'

Naomi's heart sank. It had been another long day of walking, her feet ached and her throat was dry, and having laid down her blanket she was ready to fall asleep. She forced a smile as she looked at her friend's round, cheerful face framed with a mass of black curls. 'Oh, hello, Miriam,' she replied. 'I'm going to Jerusalem, the same as you.'

'But who's running the bread store, then?' Miriam asked, her bright eyes taking in Naomi's dusty clothes and tattered shoes. 'And how is your mother travelling with her new baby?'

Naomi sighed. A few other people had already asked her this question so she had her answer ready. 'My parents aren't with me. I'm travelling with my aunt and uncle,' she lied.

'Great!' said her friend, as she settled down on her mat. 'We can travel together, then!'

'Yes, that's great!' echoed Naomi.

Soon the sound of steady breathing told Naomi that Miriam was asleep, and although she was very tired herself, she lay for a while thinking back over the four days that had passed since she had left her homeland in Syria, escaping through the gates of Damascus.

At first, she had been worried that her stepfather would discover she was missing and would come after her. Naomi knew she was very useful to the family. With her mother having just had the new baby, Naomi was the one who each day had to make the bread which was sold at the market in Damascus, as well as run errands and do the household chores. How angry he must have been when he found she had gone!

Well, she was glad it would make life difficult for him. He had made her life unbearable. Her beloved father had died so suddenly, and before she had time to realize he had gone, her mother had married his younger brother. But he was nothing like her gentle, kind father. She had hated her stepfather from the very beginning for trying to take her father's place. No one could do that, and especially not him. And after he had had a few drinks, he was violent and brutal; her body had the scars to prove it. It served him right that now he would have to do more work himself!

For a brief moment Naomi thought of her mother, and a lump came into her throat when she realized that she would never see her again. She would be angry with Naomi for stealing her purse, and there would now be more work for her to do. 'But,' Naomi reminded herself fiercely, 'at least now she'll be sorry that she didn't look after me better.'

In all probability, they wouldn't have discovered she was missing until mid-morning. Finding her bed empty, they would have assumed that she had gone to the well to fetch water, as that was her first task of the day. They would think she had met a friend and had been delayed. But by now, they would have discovered that the water flask and blanket were missing, and her mother would have found her purse gone, and they would surely have realized that she had run away.

When she had told other people in the crowd that she was with her aunt and uncle, they had believed her. They all thought she was going up to Jerusalem, as they were, to celebrate the Jewish Passover. There were hundreds of people on the road, so they had no reason to realize that she was lying, especially as it was quite normal that an eleven-year-old would rather walk with her friends than with her family.

Naomi had been very glad when they had arrived at this shelter in the desert. Some of the watering places the guide had taken them to had little water and they had had to sleep outdoors, surrounded by the animals and breathing in the dust blown up by the desert wind. But this wayside inn provided good shelter, and the well within the courtyard had plenty of water. The animals had been unloaded and they were being cared for on the ground floor, while the people had been taken upstairs to sleep.

Tomorrow was the Sabbath and so, being made up of Jews, the caravan would not move. Most of the day, Naomi would be able to rest her sore feet, drink as much water as she could, and prepare herself for the last four days' walk. It would be difficult, as they had left the smooth Roman road some miles back and the way ahead now was rough and uneven. What was left of her bread was already quite hard, but one way or another she would make it. 'I'm half way there,' she told herself, 'and I'll be able to buy fresh food once I arrive.'

Chapter three

'Look, Naomi, we're almost there!' Miriam cried, and Naomi looked up, her eyes following her friend's pointed finger. Sure enough, there on the hill in the distance she could make out the faint outline of the walls surrounding Jerusalem. The weary travellers were finding the going hard as they slowly climbed up towards the city that rose majestically in the distance ahead. But as they saw Jerusalem getting nearer, they cheered and laughed, and they began walking faster towards their destination.

Jerusalem! The place where every Jew loved to be. This was their homeland. Damascus was a beautiful city, with its ancient gardens and olive groves, but Jerusalem was more precious because it was the centre of all the hopes and dreams of the Jewish people. This was the land promised to Abraham and his descendants. Here the great King David had lived and reigned, and here, one day, the Messiah would come to rule over the nation just as David had done.

Naomi listened as the travellers at the front of the caravan broke into a song. 'I lift my eyes to the hills,' they sang. 'Where does my help come from?' Then the answer came from the travellers further back in the caravan: 'My help comes from the Lord, the Maker of heaven and earth!'

For most of the travellers, the thought of spending
a week in the holy city, celebrating the barley harvest
and remembering the time so many years before when
their forefathers had escaped from slavery in Egypt, was
wonderful. But Naomi had little interest in the festival.
Since her father had died and her mother had remarried
they had not celebrated the Jewish holidays. Her
stepfather had no interest in God. 'His god is wine,' Naomi
thought bitterly.

But now she was free. Yet she felt no joy at the
thought. In fact, at this moment Naomi could not feel
anything except her aching body, her sore feet and her dry
throat. 'What will life be like in Jerusalem for a young girl
far away from home?' she wondered. 'Will I be able to keep
safe? Will I be able to find work?'

There was now no food left in her bag; that had run
out several days ago. Miriam's family had been generous
and she was very grateful for the meals she had shared
with them. Occasionally, she had left her friends for a
few hours so as not to raise their suspicions. She had
pretended to join her aunt and uncle, but during those
hours she had gone hungry. Closer to Jerusalem she had
found fields of barley, ripe and ready to harvest, and she
had pulled a few ears of the grain to eat; that had taken
the edge off her hunger. And once she got to Jerusalem
she would be able to buy fresh bread with the money in
the purse she had kept safely in her bag.

'Almost there,' Naomi said to Miriam. 'It will be good to
stop walking!'

'Yes,' her friend agreed, her bright eyes sparkling with
excitement. 'I'm looking forward to sleeping on a bed

tonight, instead of on the dusty ground! Where are you
and your family staying, Naomi? I hope it's the same inn
we're staying at.'

'I'm not sure,' Naomi answered vaguely, wondering
herself where she would lay her head that night.

As the city walls drew closer, Naomi was able to make
out the Damascus Gate and a crowd of people standing
a short distance away near a rocky hillside. She realized
that the time had come for her to leave her friend, but
she needed to be careful. 'I should join my aunt and uncle
now,' she said.

'We'll help you to find them,' Miriam said. 'Jacob's taller
than us and will be able to spot them more easily.'

'It's all right,' Naomi said quickly, 'I can see them over
there. I must hurry to catch them.' And holding tightly
onto her bag she rapidly moved away. It would never do
for Miriam to realize that she was actually on her own.
'Bye,' she called out as she left, 'and thanks for your
company!' Stepping round two donkeys just ahead, she ran
as fast as her tired legs would let her until she was hidden
from Miriam's view.

Naomi continued to run until she was sure she was far
enough away from Miriam's family. At last she slowed
down, holding her side, which was hurting badly from her
effort, and breathing very heavily. The Damascus Gate
could now be seen clearly and she was quite close to the
crowd standing near the hill a short distance from the
gate. If she slipped in among them and waited until the
Damascus caravan had entered the city, she would then be
able to go through safely herself and find a place to hide.

Chapter four

No one in the crowd took any notice of the thin, dirty girl who joined them. They were all staring up at three objects on the top of the hill. Naomi wasn't interested in the hill. She was looking the other way, watching the procession from Damascus move slowly past and eventually disappear through the city gates.

With a sigh of relief, Naomi turned round to see what the crowd was looking at. There were three figures on the hill, and as Naomi moved closer she could see Roman soldiers standing next to them. She immediately recognized that this was a place of punishment, where criminals were nailed to wooden crosses and left hanging to die in the hot sun. She had seen this before in Damascus. The Romans were very cruel to anyone who disobeyed their rules, and she had learned from a young age that you should do all you could to stay out of trouble.

Naomi was about to turn back towards the city gate when she noticed the man on the middle cross. He somehow seemed different from the other two men. What was it? She looked harder and saw that a kind of crown made from a thorn bush had been thrust onto his head, and a notice with some words written on it was placed above him. Naomi wondered what it said.

There appeared to be two groups of people at the cross. One group was mainly made up of women, who were standing to one side, holding on to one another and sobbing quietly. The other group was more noisy, shouting insults at this man. 'If you're the Son of God, show us and come down from that cross!' called out one man, who by the look of his clothes appeared to be one of the temple priests. 'He trusts in God! Let God rescue him now!' someone else shouted. 'Come down now from the cross and we'll believe in you!' another said, laughing. A Roman soldier also taunted him: 'If you're the King of the Jews, save yourself!'

'He must have done something pretty bad,' Naomi thought, and yet, as she looked at the man, she wondered. His face was so calm and peaceful, even though it was twisted with pain, and in his eyes she thought she could see kindness and love for those who were insulting him. What a strange man! Then he looked up and spoke, and Naomi heard his words clearly above the noise. 'Father, forgive them,' he said, 'for they don't know what they're doing.' For a moment, a hush came over the people, and Naomi looked around to see who this man's father was, but there was no answer from anyone in the crowd.

This man must be a fool, Naomi decided. How could anyone forgive people who were shouting and insulting him while he was suffering agony on a Roman cross? Only weak people forgave. As for her, she was strong and she would never forgive her mother or stepfather for what they had done to her. And with these bitter thoughts in her mind, Naomi turned from the hill and walked through the Damascus Gate into Jerusalem.

Chapter five

By now, another group of travellers had entered the city and was making its way towards the inns surrounding the temple area. Naomi walked with them for a short distance, assuming—rightly—that they would be going to a well. They would all need to replenish their water bottles, and their animals, after travelling long distances across the desert, would be very thirsty.

The water in Naomi's flask had run out almost two days ago and her throat was parched and dry. It was so good to draw the cool, clear water from the well and she enjoyed a long drink before filling up her flask. Nearby was a boy selling bread to the hungry travellers and she stopped to buy a small loaf. She was disappointed to see that he had only flat bread to sell. 'Of course, it's Passover,' she thought, and remembered her father telling her the story of their ancestors having to leave Egypt in a hurry. They didn't have time to wait for their bread to rise and so they baked it on their backs in the hot sun as they escaped. 'I'll have to wait seven days for the end of Passover before I can buy a soft crusty loaf,' Naomi thought sadly as she quickly broke off a piece to eat.

Passover. What fun it had been when her father was alive, with wonderful food, laughter and singing! As she thought about this, she noticed a girl about her own age coming out of a house carrying a bag and dropping it onto the roadside outside the house. Naomi suddenly remembered how she and her mother had cleaned out the cupboards and thrown away food that had yeast in it just before the Passover feast. As quickly as she could, she moved over to where the girl had dropped the bag and picked it up. Yes! Sure enough, inside the bag were scraps of bread and cakes. These would help to see her through the next few days.

A dreadful weariness now came over Naomi. Oh, how she needed to rest! The shoes she had worn to start her journey had fallen to pieces and the soles on her second pair of shoes were beginning to wear thin. Her whole body ached with the effort of walking. Naomi realized that she desperately needed a long rest before she could plan her next step. A short distance away, she could see a garden with a grove of olive trees and she slowly made her way towards it. Here she would find a cool place to rest.

Once among the trees, Naomi spread out her blanket and lay down. It was getting quite dark now, which seemed strange as it was still only the afternoon. But Naomi was too tired to wonder why and, lying under the trees, hidden from the road, she fell into a deep sleep.

It was the middle of the night when Naomi woke up feeling very cold and hungry. She ate some more bread, wrapped herself in her blanket and curled up into a ball to keep warm. For a while she lay staring up at the full moon, thinking about what she should do for the next seven days. After that time, the people from Damascus would leave to go home and it would be safe for her to move around Jerusalem and look for work. Until then, however, she would have to keep hidden as much as possible. It would be a long week, and as she lay there Naomi felt very lonely. A picture of her mother and father came into her mind and for a while she thought of how happy they had been together and how much her parents had loved her. What would her father say if he could see her now? Tears ran down her face as she thought of him. 'Oh, why did you have to leave?' she asked; but there was no answer.

At last, Naomi drifted off to sleep once more, dreaming of happier days and sleeping until dawn arrived.

Chapter six

Naomi was not sure how many days had passed. She had decided to stay in the garden until Passover was over, only venturing out to fill her water bottle at the well. The olive trees gave shade in the daytime and shelter at night, and the spot where Naomi had settled was some way off the path. From time to time, she saw people walking through the garden, but she kept herself hidden among the trees.

On her first morning there, Naomi had woken to hear men talking nearby. She sat up cautiously and saw two Roman soldiers sitting under a tree just a short distance away. She quickly lay back down again. She couldn't risk them seeing her. The Romans were in control. They were known to be ruthless and had little time for Jewish girls. She was unsure what they would do if they saw her, but she had been taught to be afraid of them. Hiding in the shadows, she listened to them talking.

'I don't know what to make of him,' one of the soldiers said.

'Nor me,' said the other; 'he was no ordinary man.'

'You're right,' responded the first. 'Have you ever seen anyone else die like that?'

'No,' his companion agreed. 'I was there when they arrested him, you know. We were told to go to the Garden of Gethsemane at night to accompany the temple guards! I felt very uncomfortable. Didn't seem right somehow.'

'Ah well,' the first soldier said, 'it's done now. And I need to be back on duty. I've been ordered to guard the tomb, as the priests are afraid his disciples might try to steal the body.'

'OK,' said his friend, standing up and stretching. 'I'll see you later. Have a good day.'

Naomi had watched from her hiding place as the soldier walked away, and she had then waited while the other soldier sat for a while before he too stood up and walked back towards the road. She felt sure that they had been talking about that man she had seen dying on the cross the day before. She wondered what his name was.

Just a few days later she had found out. Some very excited women met in the garden. They were talking so loudly that Naomi had no difficulty hearing what they said, even though they were quite a distance away.

'It's true!' one woman cried. 'I've seen him!'

'Me too!' shouted another. 'And his twelve disciples have seen him as well! How amazing is that?'

'Incredible!' called out another. 'We saw him buried, but there's no doubt—Jesus is alive!'

'So that was his name,' Naomi thought. 'Jesus.' She had no doubt that this was the man she had seen being crucified. Could it be possible that the man she had seen dying was now alive? At that moment, she wished she had Miriam with her so that she could talk to her about it. It made no sense to her, so she promised herself that once Passover was over she would try to find out more.

Chapter seven

It was just getting light. From her hiding place in the garden Naomi watched as the long caravan slowly made its way past her towards the Damascus Gate. Passover was over and life in Jerusalem would soon return to normal. Then it would be safe for her to come out of hiding.

She stood for a long time, hidden by an olive tree, watching the families with their donkeys and camels laden down for the long walk home. Occasionally, she saw people she recognized from her home town. She strained her eyes to see if she could see Miriam and her family, but the crowd was large and she didn't see her friend. She felt a little surge of fear as she thought that soon all the people she knew would be many miles away. For a moment, she wondered if she should change her mind and return with the caravan back to Damascus—but then she remembered her stepfather's cruelty and the moment passed.

Naomi waited until mid-morning. The road in front of her was quiet now. Taking a big breath, Naomi gathered up her blanket, picked up her bag and made her way towards the centre of the city. Her first stop was the bustling market to buy fruit, fish and bread. After seven days of being alone, Naomi found it very strange now to be among the jostling crowds of noisy women all intent on getting the best prices. Once or twice, women pushed her out of the way and she saw the shopkeepers looking at her with suspicion and disgust. Looking down at herself, she realized that they must think she was a beggar with her dirty face, bedraggled hair, and clothes that she had travelled and slept in for many days. 'No one will give me a job while I'm looking like this,' she thought. 'I must buy some clean clothes.'

After buying the clothes, Naomi anxiously counted out her remaining coins. The clothes had cost more than she had expected, and then she had needed new sandals, which had left her with just a few coins for food. With the money she had left she would have enough for about three or four more days' food. She would need to find a job fairly quickly. But first, she must find a place to wash and change her clothes.

Naomi had heard that in the wealthy parts of Jerusalem there were families who lived in houses that had bathrooms. She had heard that these rooms had mosaic floors and bathtubs with warm running water, and even something called 'soap' made from animal and vegetable oil, which helped the people to get clean. Some of these homes even had bath attendants who would fetch and carry the water and towels for the family. Only the friends of Herod and people with more money than she had could afford such luxury.

Naomi could just about remember how, as a small child, she had gone to the temple in Jerusalem with her parents. Before reaching the temple they had washed in a pool near to the temple mount. If she made her way towards the temple now she would certainly find this pool.

It didn't take long for Naomi to get to the pool. She had forgotten how big and how beautiful it was! It was surrounded by pomegranate and fig trees, which gave some welcome shade. Many people were washing themselves there. Most of them were perfectly clean already, but even they needed to wash as it was a law that you couldn't enter the temple without this ritual washing.

Naomi found a quiet spot away from the people and by the water's edge. After walking down the stone steps, she jumped into the pool and was soon scrubbing herself and her clothes in the cool, clear water.

Chapter eight

How much better she felt with clean clothes on her body and new sandals on her feet! Naomi stood by the pool looking at her reflection in the water. The girl was thinner than she had been in Damascus, and the eyes that looked back at her seemed huge. But the thin face was clean and her long, dark hair was now plaited and hanging neatly down her back. Her old tunic and blanket were washed and had dried quickly in the sun. Carefully, she rolled these up and tucked them under her arm. The old sandals were left abandoned beside the pool. Perhaps she would venture a little way up towards the temple. It was a beautiful place, and maybe if she got closer, God might hear her if she asked for help to find a job.

The path leading up to the temple mount was made of steep stone steps and it took Naomi a while to climb it. Her seven days' stay in the garden with little exercise had left her legs weak, but eventually she arrived at the top and stepped onto the huge, flat courtyard. She looked around. On one side there were stalls where people were changing money or selling animals and birds for sacrifice in the temple. Wandering around this area were Jews and Gentiles and even a few Roman soldiers. Across the courtyard was the main temple itself, where only the Jews were allowed. As Naomi looked at the magnificent building, she gasped in wonder. It was so white! The stone walls dazzled so brightly in the sun that Naomi had to shield her eyes from the glare.

It was also very hot, and Naomi moved quickly into the shade of an area around the temple courts that was supported by great marble pillars. Ahead of her was a little group of people who were singing a beautiful song. She moved towards them and sat down against one of the pillars nearby to listen. She felt the joyful melody of the song soothe her hurting heart, and for a little while she felt at peace.

She must have dozed off, for she was suddenly aware that the little group had stopped singing and the members were talking together in excited voices.

'I thought it was my imagination when I saw Jesus,' one of the women said, 'but then I found out that my sister and brother had seen him too!'

'He came to our home,' said a man. 'It was incredible! He sat down just as he had done when he was alive and had a meal with us!'

'He was the same, and yet he was so different,' another said.

'Thomas asked to see the nail prints in his hands, you know,' someone added, 'and Thomas said that he even saw the scar the spear had made in his side!'

'Tell the others what happened, Peter, when you saw Jesus by the lakeside!' another person said, and the whole group stopped talking and turned to look at the man at the centre of the group.

Naomi moved closer to them so that she could hear more clearly. Although these people spoke the same language as her, they had a different accent, which made it a bit difficult to understand.

'Well,' the man they had called Peter began quietly, 'you all know how I let Jesus down when he was arrested. What a coward I was! I followed the soldiers as they took him to the high priest's palace, but I was too scared to get very close. I stood by the fire, warming my hands, and watched from a distance. Three times people asked me if I was a friend of Jesus, and three times I said I didn't even know him! I felt so ashamed afterwards. I had let down my friend when he needed me most! Then they killed him, and I wished that I could die too. But after three days he came back to life! I was so happy—but I felt sure he would never trust me again!

'Then I was fishing with James and John and we saw him,' Peter continued. 'I jumped out of the boat and swam to the shore. It really was him! He had lit a fire and we cooked some of the fish we'd caught and had breakfast together. Then Jesus spoke to me. He was so kind.'

Peter paused for a moment and drew a deep breath. 'He said nothing about how I'd let him down—he just asked me to follow him and to help others to follow him too! Why he should forgive me I'll never understand!'

So Jesus was alive! At least, that was what his friends were saying. And once again there was talk about forgiveness. What about fairness and justice? There must have been a reason why he had been put to death. Bad people should be punished; you couldn't just pretend that what they had done hadn't happened. Naomi didn't belong with these people.

Feeling suddenly quite depressed, she left the shade of the porch. She kicked a loose stone at the top of the steps and watched it fall before slowly making her way down from the temple mount and back on to the road below. At the bottom she straightened her back. 'I really must find a job,' she thought to herself.

Chapter nine

'Excuse me, sir,' Naomi said, and the large, round man who was busy selling bread turned to look down at the young girl who was speaking.

'Yes, child? How many bread rolls do you want?' he asked.

'Oh no, I don't want bread, thank you—I'm looking for work,' Naomi replied. 'I know how to make bread and can work very fast.'

Naomi had lost count of the number of shopkeepers she had approached with the same request over the past few days. So far, none of them had offered her work and she was beginning to despair. Some guessed that she wasn't from Jerusalem because she spoke Aramaic with a different accent and they were suspicious of her. She had gone first to the rich homes around Mount Zion asking if they needed workers in their kitchens, but without any success. Then she had tried at the inns and shops. The trouble was that the Passover pilgrims had left Jerusalem so there were few visitors in the city now. 'Wait until Pentecost, when the visitors come back,' some people told her. 'Then there will be work.' But Pentecost was weeks away, and Naomi had already run out of money for food.

The large man was still looking down at Naomi. 'How old are you, child?' he asked.

'I'm twelve,' she lied. 'And I'm not a child, I'm old enough to work!'

The man leaned closer to her. 'You run along home, little girl. It'll soon be dark and your mother will be wondering where you are. Come back in a couple of years and I might be able to find you a job.'

As Naomi turned away, he caught sight of tears in her eyes and he quickly thrust a bread roll into her hand. 'Here, eat this. I've a feeling you need it,' he added kindly.

Naomi did need it. She hadn't eaten all day and was feeling quite weak with hunger. She walked for a while and then sat down beside the road to eat the bread. A short distance from her sat a beggar. He was blind, and from time to time he called out to people passing by, asking them for money. Occasionally, people stopped and put a coin into his bowl. 'That's what I'll have to do soon,' Naomi thought.

As she sat eating her bread and watching the beggar, a plan formed in her mind. She finished her bread, had a long drink from her water bottle and stood up. Slowly, and very softly, the girl moved towards the beggar until she was in front of him. She looked up and down the road. There was no one near to see her. Quickly and very quietly, so that the blind man wouldn't hear her, she reached down and took two shiny coins from his bowl. Then she turned and fled down the road.

Panting hard, Naomi finally stopped beside a well to catch her breath. She didn't feel proud of what she had done. 'But,' she told herself, 'he didn't know, and anyway, he still had one coin left in his bowl.' The two coins might buy her a piece of bread and a small fish, which meant that tomorrow she wouldn't starve. And tonight she would sleep in a cosy barn she had found a few nights before. The barn belonged to a rich person who lived on the slope of Mount Zion and she could creep in after dark without the owner seeing her. It was a good place, as the donkeys were well looked after and given fresh hay each day, and she had managed to make herself a little place to sleep in a corner out of the wind.

Chapter ten

Over the next few days, Naomi got into a routine of getting up early and leaving the barn before the household awoke. Then she would go out looking for food. She would go to the food market to pick up pieces of fish or fruit that had fallen from the market stalls. Sometimes, she found food that had been left behind by rich families having picnics in the grounds of one of the grand buildings built by Herod. This was the king they had called 'Herod the Great'. He was dead now, and one of his sons was supposed to be looking after the needs of the Jewish people, although Naomi remembered her father saying that he was more interested in being friendly with the enemy—the Romans—than in caring for them.

On occasions, when the shopkeepers weren't looking, Naomi would steal from their stalls. And when she could find food no other way, Naomi took money given to beggars. She had to make sure no one was looking, take a coin or two and then run! One place she had found quite profitable was the entrance to the temple. Many beggars sat there to ask people for money as they came into the temple. Religious Jews believed that they could please God by giving to the poor, so, as they went up to the temple to pray, they would throw money to the beggars sitting by the path.

Naomi had considered begging herself, but she knew she would draw too much attention to herself. The temple officials might begin to ask her questions and she knew that children with no parents could be taken and forced to do jobs in the temple that no one else wanted to do, such as cleaning up the blood of animals after they had been killed for the sacrifices. Or she might be sold to one of the rich folk as a slave and have to work for no money and little food.

There was one man who always seemed to get given a good number of silver and gold coins. On several occasions, Naomi had looked into his tin tray and seen the pile of coins there. She had frequently walked past him, hoping for the opportunity to take some, but there were always too many people around. She could see that he was unable to walk as his legs were bent and thin. Every morning, his friends carried him to this place called the 'Beautiful' gate, which led into the temple courts, and each evening, they carried him home again.

For two days, Naomi had only managed to find a few pieces of stale bread and she was starting to feel very weak and hungry again. She decided to go to the temple area to see if she could take some of the lame man's coins. It was afternoon and the hottest part of the day, the time when many people rested. There were no worshippers going into the temple, and as she approached, Naomi could see the beggar dozing in the sun. This was her chance! Checking there was no one about, she quietly crept towards him.

Silently, she reached out her thin arm and grasped a handful of the coins. But as she did so, the coins clinked against one another and the man woke up with a start. 'What!' he roared. 'You little thief!' and he grasped the stick beside him and swung it at Naomi, striking her hand that held the money. With a cry of pain, Naomi dropped the coins and for a moment stared into the man's accusing eyes. She would have picked up the coins from the ground where they had dropped, but at that moment two men who had heard the man's cry came towards them to see what was happening. Naomi fled, crying with frustration and pain as she ran.

Chapter eleven

That night, Naomi crept into her little bed in the barn feeling very sorry for herself. Her hand was now red and swollen and her empty stomach was complaining loudly. The donkeys had been given some leftover vegetables from the house and Naomi managed to find a few morsels they had missed. She also found an egg laid by one of the chickens that occasionally wandered into the barn, and she ate that too, even though it was raw. It smelled and tasted funny, and Naomi thought it must have been there some time, but it was better than nothing. 'That will have to do today,' the girl thought sadly, and nursing her painful hand she curled herself up in her blanket and fell into a troubled sleep.

In the middle of the night, Naomi woke sensing that all was not well. Her hand was throbbing and her head was very hot. As she moved to get more comfortable, she felt a sharp pain in her stomach. 'I'm ill,' she whispered to herself. 'What am I to do?'

For the first time since running away, she wished she had stayed at home. 'If only Mother was here,' poor Naomi thought. 'She would look after me.' And there in that cold barn, far away from her mother, she felt the tears rolling down her hot cheeks. 'How silly I was to think I could look after myself!' she thought. 'I'm going to die here, and no one will know or care!'

When morning came, Naomi was worse. One minute she felt hot, but the next she was shivering with cold. She was vaguely aware of the cock crowing to let her know that it was time to get up. Soon the household would be awake and by then she should have left the barn. But she was too weak to move, so she lapsed into a troubled sleep again. She groaned whenever she rolled onto her painful hand, and a chicken clucked in sympathy. From time to time, she was aware of the sounds of movements in the house, and once or twice people came into the barn to see to the animals, but curled up in the corner she was too ill to worry or care.

Naomi had no idea how long she lay there, drifting in and out of consciousness. She found she was having some very strange dreams. At one point, she thought she saw her friend's brother, Jacob, bending over her, his brown eyes wide with shock. Then she thought she heard her friend Miriam say, 'Is it really her?' When she had the sensation of being lifted up and carried, she thought she must be dying, and she wondered vaguely what happened to children when they died.

Chapter twelve

When she awoke, Naomi found that she was lying on a proper bed with a pillow and was covered with a soft white blanket. With great difficulty and pain she managed to raise her head, and she saw that she was in a small room with white painted walls and a window through which the sun was shining. A jug of clean water and a towel were beside her bed. She saw that there was another bed in the room; it was empty, and she wondered who slept there.

She could hear two female voices chatting quietly together in another room, and she could also hear the sounds of a donkey being led past her window. Naomi struggled to think. Where was she? And how long had she been here? She lifted her arm to rub her eyes and saw that her hand was wrapped up in a bandage—how had she hurt it? But it was all too hard for her to remember, and with a moan she dropped her head back onto the soft pillow.

'She's waking up, Mother,' a voice cried out, and a woman came running into the room. 'Thank God!' the woman said. Naomi recognized the voices of her friend Miriam and Miriam's mother Hannah, but her brain told her she must be imagining things. But then she saw the two anxious faces looking down at her and realized that her ears were telling the truth.

'Where am I?' she asked weakly.

'You're in Jerusalem, dear,' Hannah replied, 'and you've been very ill.'

'I don't understand,' Naomi said. 'You should be in Damascus!'

'It's you who should be in Damascus!' Miriam exclaimed, tucking her black curls behind her ears so that she could see her friend more clearly. 'Why didn't you go back with the others? And how did you get into our barn? If Jacob hadn't found you when he did, you'd be dead by now!'

'Hush, dear,' Hannah said to her daughter. 'There'll be plenty of time to talk when Naomi is feeling a bit better. The important thing now is to get some food into her and to let her sleep. Run into the kitchen and pour out a cup of the chicken soup I made.'

Gently, Hannah put her hand under Naomi's head and raised her up so that she could drink from the cup which her friend brought her. The broth tasted so good that she drank to the very bottom of the cup before Hannah settled her back down again. 'Now go to sleep, my dear. When you're feeling better we can find out what this is all about.'

Chapter thirteen

Over the next few days, Naomi was able to piece together what had happened to her. It seemed that the barn where she had chosen to sleep belonged to a man called Saul. Apparently, he was a well-known Jewish student of the law who came from a town called Tarsus and who was in Jerusalem to learn from Gamaliel, a famous teacher in the temple. Saul had been looking for a couple to take care of his house while he was in Jerusalem, and Hannah and her husband, Jeremiah, had been offered the job when they met him in the temple during Passover.

'It's a very good job,' Miriam explained to her friend. 'I help Mother with the housework, and Father and Jacob look after the animals. Master Saul pays well and he's helping Jacob with his studies, too, so we're happy that we decided to stay in Jerusalem.'

When she heard why Naomi had decided to leave Damascus, Miriam was full of sympathy. She was amazed to hear of her friend's adventures. 'Weren't you afraid to be all alone in Jerusalem?' she asked, her eyes wide with admiration.

'I was a bit scared,' Naomi admitted, 'but only when I found that no one would give me a job; then I knew I was in trouble. How lucky I chose your barn to sleep in!'

Her friend agreed. 'But my mother says there's no such thing as luck. She says God brought you to us.'

Naomi gave an unhappy smile. 'If there is a God, he certainly doesn't care about me,' she said.

Hannah had been horrified to hear how Naomi had run away from home. 'Your poor mother!' she exclaimed, fingering the necklace that she always wore round her neck. 'She must be worried sick!'

Naomi's eyes filled with tears as she realized that this was true, but her response was bitter. 'She's too busy with her baby and her horrid husband to worry about me,' she said.

'Well, that may be how it seems to you,' Hannah said gently, 'but I'm sure she loves you very much, although she may not have shown it because of being so sad and tired.'

'But that was her own fault,' Naomi said angrily. 'She shouldn't have married that man! I'll never forgive her for that.'

Miriam's mother sighed. 'We can't always do what we want to do, dear,' she said, patting down the pillow behind Naomi. The girl wondered what she meant. Hannah continued firmly, 'Anyway, we must find a way to get a message to your mother to tell her you're safe.' With this, she bustled off to make their evening meal.

That evening, Hannah discussed the dilemma with her husband, Jeremiah. He agreed that a message should be sent with the next caravan leaving Jerusalem for Damascus. There was likely to be a group taking leather goods to Damascus very soon. It was important that they got news to Rebecca, Naomi's mother, as soon as possible, reassuring her that her daughter was alive and well. They would send Jacob the following morning with a message.

Chapter fourteen

'Now, take good care of Naomi,' Hannah told her daughter. 'She's been very ill and mustn't get overtired.'

'OK, Mother,' Miriam said happily. 'We'll walk slowly and stop for a rest now and then. And if the olives are ripe, we'll bring some back with us. Come on, Naomi! I'll carry the picnic!'

Naomi had taken short walks with her friend over the past days in and around the city of Jerusalem. She had made a few trips to the market and had even walked with Jacob to the temple, but today she and Miriam were going further. The plan was to walk through Jerusalem and out towards the Mount of Olives. There they would sit under the trees, admiring the view across Jerusalem, and eat the picnic prepared by Hannah. There was freshly made bread, which Naomi had helped to make, and some fried fish, olives, walnuts, and some sweet oranges picked from a tree in the garden. 'What a feast!' Naomi said, as she watched Miriam packing the food. And how different from the food she had eaten when she first arrived in Jerusalem, she thought.

Chatting happily together, the two girls set off down the hill towards the city. From time to time, they would pick up news in the market of the happenings in

Jerusalem. There were still rumours about Jesus having come back to life, and Miriam was certain they were true. She said that she herself had seen him talking to a group of followers. Naomi wasn't so sure. 'He was talking about the kingdom of heaven and why he had to die,' Miriam explained. 'I didn't understand much, but I'm sure it was him! And lots of other people have seen him,' she added. 'Not just one or two—hundreds!'

Naomi was too happy to argue with her friend. The sun was shining, the air was cool and clear, and today she was free to walk and play. Once she was well she would be able to help Hannah with her work, but for now she could enjoy feeling safe and being with friends who cared about her. She grabbed Miriam's hand and together they ran to the bottom of the hill and through the market square towards the city centre.

From time to time, the girls stopped for a rest and a drink of water, and it wasn't long before the road began to climb upwards again. The sounds of the city were now just a faint murmur in the background and the path was more winding and rough. On the slopes of the Mount of Olives were trees and shrubs, and occasionally they would see a goat chewing contentedly on an overhanging branch. Almost at the top of the mount, Miriam stopped and turned off the path. She bent down and pushed her way past a low-hanging branch to reach a flat piece of ground beneath an olive tree. 'This is the perfect place for our picnic!' she exclaimed, and threw herself onto the ground, her black curls bobbing up and down.

'It's perfect,' Naomi agreed.

What a feast they had! 'Food always tastes better outside, doesn't it?' Naomi said, as she happily bit into the tasty fish.

'Yes!' laughed Miriam. 'Especially when there is no one around to tell you not to eat so fast, or to talk with your mouth full!'

All too soon the picnic was over and the friends lay back with a sigh, looking up into the overhanging branches and lazily watching the movement of the leaves above them.

Chapter fifteen

'Wake up, Naomi! Oh do please wake up!' Naomi opened her eyes to see her friend standing over her, shaking with excitement. The effort of the long walk and the comfortable feeling of a full stomach had sent her right off to sleep, but now she was being rudely awakened by Miriam.

'Oh,' she said blearily, 'I must have fallen asleep.'

'You certainly did, and I didn't want to wake you, but I just had to!' Miriam said, speaking in a loud whisper. 'You see, he's here!'

'Who's here? Where?' Naomi asked, rubbing her eyes and trying to make sense of her friend's chatter. She could see a small group of men gathered at the top of the mount, quite near to them. They must have walked right past her as she slept.

'Jesus!' Miriam said. 'He just walked past with his disciples! Do wake up, Naomi, so that you can see him!'

Reluctantly, Naomi got up from her comfortable spot. Seeing her friend jumping up and down with impatience, she tried to gather together her muddled thoughts and follow her through the trees where they could get a better view.

Hidden there among the trees, they had a clear view of the little group. There were about eleven men gathered

around the man in the centre. One of the men Naomi
recognized. He had been in the temple and was the one
they had called Peter. The man in the middle was Jesus.
He looked different from the suffering man she had seen
on the cross, but there was no mistaking it: he was the
same man, only today his face was calm and smiling.
Naomi shivered. Was this real? Perhaps she was still
asleep.

As the girls crouched down to peer through the
branches of the olive trees, they heard one of the men ask
Jesus a question. 'Has the day come for you to be crowned
as king?' There was a silence as everyone waited for his
reply.

'God will decide when that day will be,' Jesus said at
last. 'I'm going back to my Father and you won't see me.
But you will receive power when the Holy Spirit comes on
you, and you will be my witnesses, first here in Jerusalem,
then to the whole world.'

The girls then saw Jesus raise his hands and say
something very quietly to the disciples. As they strained
to hear they saw, to their utter amazement, that Jesus
seemed to float up into the air and disappear behind a low
cloud!

Naomi rubbed her eyes. This must be a dream! People
don't just float away like that! But the disciples were
staring up into the sky where Jesus had disappeared. If
she was in a dream, so were they! She looked at Miriam,
who was standing open-mouthed beside her. When she
turned to look back at the disciples, she let out a gasp.
Now there were two new men in white clothes standing
with the group and speaking to them. 'Why are you

looking up into the sky?' they asked the disciples. 'This same Jesus who has been taken from you into heaven will come back in the same way you have seen him go.'

The girls were speechless. They watched as the two strange men in white disappeared as quickly as they had come. They watched as the cloud that had hidden Jesus moved away, showing nothing but a clear blue sky. And they watched as the eleven men with bright shining faces turned to one another, all talking at the same time, and then hurried past them on the path back down towards Jerusalem.

Chapter sixteen

'Well, it all sounds like a lot of nonsense to me,' Jacob said when the girls returned home. Miriam had told the story to her father, to her mother and now to Jacob. Jeremiah had just said, 'Hmm,' scratching the bald patch on the top of his head, as he always did when he was unsure what to say. Hannah had pressed her hands together as if in prayer and exclaimed, 'How wonderful!' Jacob, however, had showed total disbelief. Naomi had said nothing at all. She was still not at all sure what she had seen. Her mind was in a whirl.

'Ask Naomi!' Miriam insisted. 'She was there and saw it too!'

Jacob turned to Naomi. 'Well, Naomi, what did you see?'

Naomi went pale. She admired Jacob very much. He was very clever, and since being in Jerusalem he had learned a lot in his lessons from Saul and the priests at the temple. If he thought the story was nonsense, it probably was. 'I really don't know what I saw,' she said painfully. 'I'd been asleep and I may have been dreaming … It's all just such a muddle.' She rubbed her hand over her forehead as if to clear her head, and immediately Hannah stepped forward and took her hand.

'You're exhausted, child,' she said. 'You must go straight to bed.' And Naomi was only too willing to go.

She lay quietly in her bed, listening to the discussion going on in the next room. What a strange and exciting day it had been! It was true, she thought she had seen the man—Jesus—disappear. But how could that be? What did it all mean? She could hear Miriam's excited voice explaining every detail of their day, and she could also hear Jacob telling Miriam that she was a silly girl who lived in a world of make-believe.

As she listened, she knew that she didn't want to believe that she had seen Jesus. If it really was him, he must be someone really special, and this gave her an uncomfortable feeling. She remembered the words she had heard when he was on the cross: 'Father, forgive them.' Well, she didn't understand how you could forgive people who had hurt you—especially when they weren't even sorry. She couldn't forgive her mother and stepfather, and, what was more, she didn't want to forgive them, either.

It seemed only a few minutes later that Hannah crept into the room. All was quiet in the rest of the house. The discussions had stopped and the men were outside, cleaning the barn and feeding the donkeys. Miriam was busy preparing vegetables for the evening meal for when Saul returned from his studies at the temple. He always had other important men with him. One was called a scribe; his job was to write down the things that Saul was learning so that he could read them to him later.

'I see you've had a good sleep,' Hannah said quietly to Naomi as she sat down beside her. 'That's good. I think perhaps Miriam took you too far this morning, so you must take it easy for the rest of the day.'

Naomi smiled up at Hannah. 'Thank you,' she said gratefully.

Hannah took a deep breath. 'Naomi, I need to tell you that we sent a message to your mother and have just received a reply ... Now, don't look so frightened, child,' she added quickly, as Naomi quickly sat up in bed, her hands clutching at the bedclothes and her eyes wide with fear. 'Your mother has been so worried about you! We've told her you're safe and asked if we can keep you here with us for a while.'

'What did she say?' Naomi asked anxiously.

Hannah smiled. 'She said that she loves you and only wants you to be safe and happy.'

Naomi's eyes filled with tears. For so long she had wanted to hear those words from her mother, and now, she thought, she was hearing them too late. 'Don't make me go back to Damascus,' she whispered to Hannah, who replied gently, 'You can stay with us for as long as you need to, my dear.'

Chapter seventeen

For the next few days, Miriam and Naomi took only short walks from the house, on Hannah's orders. The girls didn't talk about what they had seen on the Mount of Olives and Naomi was glad. She also felt a nagging anxiety that, now that her mother knew where she was, she might come to Jerusalem to insist she return home. 'But she doesn't really care about me,' she thought to herself, 'so why would she bother to come all the way here to get me?' All the same, she felt safer when she was with Hannah, and she now spent more of her time helping in the kitchen. 'You certainly know how to make excellent bread,' Hannah told her, and Naomi was pleased.

On this particular morning, Hannah, with the help of Naomi and Miriam, was packing a basket with bread rolls, fish and olives to take to Saul and the men who were with him at the temple. They had been studying there all morning. Today the subject was Pentecost, and they were learning about the time 1,400 years before when God gave Moses the Ten Commandments. Gamaliel was an expert in Jewish history and everyone respected him very much. They called him Rabban Gamaliel, which Jacob said meant 'Our Teacher'.

'Come, girls,' Hannah said, 'let's go together to the temple today—the walk will do us all good!' Naomi was feeling stronger now, and Hannah was pleased to see that she had put on weight and had a healthy colour in her cheeks. How pale and ill she had been when they found her! Hannah would not easily forget that thin face and body with stick-like arms and legs that could hardly hold her weight.

By the time the three had gone down the hill, through the city and climbed back up to the temple on the other side, they were ready for a rest. The men's lesson had not quite finished so Hannah and the two girls sat down to rest in the cool shade in the area around the temple courts. They leaned against the great marble pillars and silently took in the beautiful sight of the temple in front of them.

When Naomi saw a group of people singing nearby, she realized it was the same place where she had sat all those weeks before.

'What lovely singing!' Hannah said. 'I wonder who these people are? Listen to how they are praising God!'

'They're followers of Jesus!' Miriam said quickly. 'I recognize some of them from that day on the Mount of Olives. Let's move closer.'

Hannah and Miriam quickly moved a little nearer to the group, with Naomi following more reluctantly. She remembered how happy the group had been when she had seen them before, but today they were absolutely bubbling over with happiness. For some reason, their smiling faces and sweet, joyful singing made her feel very depressed.

All of a sudden, the singing stopped and one of the men in the group said, 'Let's pray the prayer Jesus taught us.' Then the little group all began to pray together. It was a strange prayer. It began, 'Our Father in heaven'. All the prayers Naomi had heard before began with 'Blessed are you, Lord our God, King of the universe', or something like that. The only time she could remember a prayer about God being Father was at her own father's funeral. What had they called that prayer? Something beginning with K ... Ka- something. Oh yes, Kaddish, that was it. They had had to say that for seven days after her father's funeral. It was supposed to help—but it hadn't helped her at all. And what was the use of a father far away in heaven?

Naomi thought sadly about her own father and how lonely she felt without him. She remembered his short illness and how suddenly he had died, leaving her and her mother alone. 'But we were all right,' she thought to herself bitterly, remembering how she and her mother had managed to keep the bakery business going. 'How glad I am that I have such a wonderful daughter!' her mother used to say. Naomi had felt so close to her mother then. 'We were all right until *he* arrived to spoil everything,' Naomi thought.

'And forgive us our sins, as we forgive those who sin against us,' the group were chanting, and in disgust Naomi stood up and moved away. 'If they knew what I've been through,' she thought angrily, 'they wouldn't say such stupid things.'

At that moment, Jacob appeared beside her. 'What are you looking so angry about, Naomi?' he asked, smiling down at her.

'Oh, hello, Jacob,' Naomi said a little shyly, and then she blurted out, 'It's those crazy people with all their talk about a father in heaven and forgiveness. It makes me sick!'

Chapter eighteen

The number of people in Jerusalem was increasing each day now as people gathered for the festival of Pentecost. Saul and the men of the house were spending more time than usual at the temple, helping the priests to manage the large number of visitors coming to worship. So, when a large, red-faced man came puffing up the path towards Saul's house one day, only the ladies were there to meet him. When he appeared quite suddenly at the kitchen door, three pairs of startled eyes looked up from their vegetable-peeling to stare at him.

There was a stunned silence, and then everything happened at once. Naomi dropped her knife onto the kitchen table and ran out as fast as she could. The man reached out to try to grab her as she passed, but she was too quick for him. Wildly she pushed past him and ran into the yard outside. 'It's him!' cried Miriam. 'The wicked stepfather!' and she rushed out in pursuit of her friend.

After the shock of seeing him, Hannah regained her composure and politely asked him to sit down. As calmly as she could, she poured him a drink of water and suggested he stay until the men returned from the temple. After a few minutes, Miriam returned and glared angrily at the man before retreating into the back room. Hannah sat quietly, her hands playing with her necklace to keep herself calm while they waited. Of Naomi there was no sign. She had disappeared.

It seemed an age before Jeremiah and Jacob returned. They too were shocked to see Naomi's stepfather.

'I've come to take my daughter home,' said the man, whose name was Jude. He spoke in a harsh voice, which made Jacob want to hit him.

'I'm sorry, sir,' Jeremiah said quietly, 'I don't think I can let you do that.'

'Her mother wants her home,' Jude continued more loudly, 'and you have no right to keep the girl here.'

'Then Rebecca must come and collect her herself,' Jeremiah said firmly, and Hannah felt very proud of her husband.

'Well, she can't come herself,' the man continued. 'She is soon to have another child, and she needs Naomi to help look after the boy.'

'I'm sorry, sir, but I cannot agree to you taking her. She's happy here and we have promised her mother to take care of her,' Jeremiah said.

Naomi's stepfather stood up, towering over Jeremiah. 'How dare you!' he shouted. 'I demand that you let me take the girl! You have no right to keep her here as your slave!'

Now Jacob stood up. He was a little taller than Jeremiah and at that moment felt very brave. 'Don't you threaten my father!' he shouted back. 'You have no right to come here and tell us how to treat a member of the family. It was you who drove Naomi away. We know you're nothing but a bully! Get out of our house before I get the guards to throw you out!'

Jude sank back into his chair, breathing heavily, and Jacob, white with rage, sat down as well, not taking his eyes off the man. Hannah was very still in the corner, her hands clasped tightly together, while Miriam peeped through the doorway from the back room, her eyes wide with admiration for her brother.

After a moment, Jude spoke again, more quietly this time. 'Very well,' he said. 'I warned Rebecca that her daughter was nothing but trouble, but I said I would try to get her back. At the very least, let me see Naomi so that I can tell Rebecca she's OK.'

Jeremiah looked at Hannah with a question in his eyes, and she said, 'If Naomi is willing to come in, then let Jude see her. But we cannot let him take her away. I've promised she can stay as long as she needs to.'

Jeremiah turned to Miriam, who stood in the doorway shaking her head, her curls falling across her face. 'Miriam, please will you go and ask Naomi if she will come and see her stepfather? Tell her that she is not leaving us.'

'I don't know where she's gone,' Miriam cried in agitation. 'She was so afraid, she just ran. She could be anywhere by now, and we may never see her again. And it's all his fault,' she added, pointing at Jude. For the first time since he had arrived, Jude looked worried.

'She can't have gone far,' he said.

'Is that what you said when she ran from home last time?' Jacob asked with a sneer. 'Wait here,' he continued, turning towards the door. 'I think I know where she might be.'

A moment later he was back, holding the hand of a very frightened Naomi. 'She was hiding in the barn,' Jacob explained, and turning to Jude he continued, 'Now, say what you have to say and then go.'

'Are you all right, child?' Naomi's stepfather asked.

She lifted her head defiantly. 'I'm fine, thank you, and I'm staying here.'

'Have you a message for your mother?' he asked again, and Naomi shook her head.

Hannah spoke up. 'Naomi, I'm sure your mother would be happier about you being here if you could send her a message.'

Naomi gulped. 'Tell her that I miss her and hope she is well, but that I can't come home until, until ...' she tailed off.

Jeremiah stood up. 'I'm afraid we must ask you to leave now,' he said to Jude politely but firmly. 'You've seen that Naomi is well. Perhaps when Rebecca is able to travel she could come herself to stay with us. Please tell her she would be very welcome.'

Chapter nineteen

E veryone agreed that the ladies should not be left
alone in the house during the next few days until
the festival of Pentecost was over. Jerusalem was full of
people from many countries around Israel and it would be
all too easy for Jude to take Naomi and hide in the crowd.
When Jacob had lessons with Saul, Jeremiah would stay
at home with them. At other times, when Jeremiah had to
carry out duties for the household, Jacob would stay there.

'I'm sure he won't come back,' Hannah reassured
Naomi, 'but we must take particular care of you until the
festival is over and the caravan returns to Damascus.'

The Day of Pentecost had arrived. Jacob was sitting
with the girls at the kitchen door watching a constant
stream of laughing, chattering people going to the temple.
There they would read the books of Moses and thank God
for giving them the Law. It was also the time when they
celebrated the wheat harvest, when the workers would be
in the fields gathering in the ripe seeds ready to make into
flour for bread.

Some of the people were carrying beautiful baskets
of grapes, figs, pomegranates, olives or dates with them.
These were farmers, Jacob explained, who kept the first
lot of fruit they had picked to take to the temple to thank
God for the harvest.

'Do you think it would be OK for us to go with them?' Miriam asked her brother. 'I'd love to join the celebration!'

Jacob thought for a moment. 'I suppose if we keep together and watch out for Naomi it should be all right. What do you think, Naomi?'

'I'd like to go,' she said, blushing with pleasure at Jacob's concern for her, 'but do you think it's safe?'

'Of course we'll be safe with Jacob,' Miriam said proudly. 'You should have heard him stand up to your stepfather! It was amazing!'

Jacob got to his feet, embarrassed. 'Come on then, you two, let's go,' he said quickly.

Jerusalem was full of people. Some were coming back from the temple, while others were going towards it. Many were singing, others were laughing and dancing, and the children were running and playing together. Naomi, protected by her two friends, was happy to be part of it all.

But something very strange indeed was happening. It was as they got closer to the temple gate that they heard it. It sounded like a really strong wind coming from the upstairs of a house just across the road. The strange thing was that they didn't feel any wind—they just heard it. The noisy crowd stopped and turned to look at the upstairs window where the sound was coming from. Through the window, Naomi was astonished to see what looked like a flame of fire on top of a man's head.

'Did you see that?' she whispered to Miriam, who nodded, wide-eyed, putting her fingers to her lips.

The watching crowd were silent as they listened first to the sound of the wind dying down, and then to the noise of those in the house shouting for joy. Then the people in the house emerged through the front door and came out into the street, and the girls recognized them as Jesus's followers, the ones they had seen on the Mount of Olives. The flames of fire had disappeared now, but their faces were glowing!

What happened then was very confusing. First one man spoke, then another. They seemed to be bubbling over with excitement and happiness. Jacob, Miriam and Naomi moved closer so that they could hear what the men were saying.

'Listen! Can you hear that?' Miriam asked breathlessly. 'That man is speaking in our language!'

'Yes, but that's impossible!' Naomi gasped. 'He's not from Syria!'

'And listen to that one!' Miriam continued. 'What language is he speaking?'

The most amazing fact was that all the people in the crowd, no matter what country they came from, understood perfectly what these men were saying! Being from Galilee, the disciples of Jesus usually spoke their own dialect of Aramaic, but now they were praising God quite clearly in the Syrian dialect, and Naomi recognized the language of her town. She could see as she looked around the crowd that everyone else could understand too—even those from Greece and Persia! She heard a man exclaim, 'How can it be that we can hear the wonderful works of God in our own language?' And everyone agreed that it was the strangest thing they had ever heard.

Then the people all started talking at once. Someone shouted, 'They're drunk!' and Jacob agreed. 'They must have had too much wine,' he said. 'Look at them, shouting and laughing!'

But Naomi was not so sure. She knew what her stepfather looked like when he was drunk. And his speech became slurred and muddled, not like the speech of these men. 'How can they be drunk?' she asked. 'They're talking quite clearly.'

Just then Peter, the leader of the group, stood up to speak, and the crowd surged forward to hear what he had to say. 'We're not drunk!' he shouted. 'It's only nine o'clock in the morning! We'll tell you what has happened. Do you remember how the old prophet, years ago, said that one day God would pour out his Holy Spirit on his children? Well, it's happened; and I'll tell you why!'

'I'm not standing here listening to this rubbish,' Jacob snorted, turning away. 'Let's go home.'

'Oh, please wait just a minute, Jacob,' Miriam pleaded. 'I want to know why this has happened.'

Jacob rolled his eyes, but stayed still as Peter went on.

'Only a few weeks ago at Passover, you people helped to drive Jesus to his death. You and your leaders crucified him! He was a wonderful teacher and showed by the powerful things he did that he came from God. But his death was part of God's wonderful plan! He didn't die because he deserved to, he died for our sins! And that wasn't all! God raised him back to life again! He is the promised Messiah!'

The girls didn't hear the end of Peter's speech, because when Jacob heard Peter accusing them of killing Jesus he had heard enough. 'Those men are mad,' he assured the girls as they walked back home. 'They are trying to persuade us that this Jesus was the Messiah, the one promised to set Israel free. How can a dead man get rid of the Romans?"

Chapter twenty

For several weeks after the strange happenings at Pentecost there were rumours around Jerusalem about thousands of people becoming followers of the new group. There were also many stories about miracles and people being healed.

The family at Saul's house was divided. Miriam and Hannah thought that the happenings in Jerusalem were wonderful and that Jesus was God's Messiah-King. Jacob was certain that the followers of Jesus were crazy fanatics. And Naomi was confused. On the one hand, she had seen and heard things that made her think that Jesus was someone pretty special. On the other hand, Jacob was a student in the temple and understood these things much better than the rest of them did. He must be right.

Jeremiah was cautious. 'Saul says that these people are dangerous,' he warned his wife. 'He is our employer, so you must keep your thoughts to yourself. He wants to keep the Jewish faith pure and has no time for Jesus or his followers. Please be careful what you say.'

'Very well,' Hannah agreed. 'No more talk about who Jesus was.'

'Or is,' insisted Miriam, adding hastily as Jeremiah frowned at her, 'OK, no more talk.'

Naomi was glad. Whenever Jesus was mentioned, she felt uncomfortable.

Since the end of the festival, and now Naomi's stepfather had returned to Damascus with the other travellers, everyone had become more relaxed. Once Naomi and Miriam had done their jobs for Hannah each morning they were free again to wander the streets around Jerusalem.

'I never want to go back to Damascus,' Naomi told her friend as they wandered down to the market one day.

'It's fun here,' Miriam agreed, 'but don't you miss all the juicy apricots and pomegranates? Jerusalem doesn't have as many fruit trees as Damascus.'

'That's true,' Naomi agreed, 'but I could never bear to live with my mother and stepfather again.'

'Don't you miss your mother?' Miriam asked.

'Of course,' Naomi said sadly, 'but I'll never forgive her for the way she let that man hurt me.'

'Why did she marry your stepfather?' her friend asked out of curiosity.

'I've no idea,' Naomi replied. 'I said to her that if we couldn't have Father, we'd manage alone.'

'And what did she say to that?' Miriam enquired.

Her friend answered, 'Mother said, "It's not right for a woman not to have a husband"—and after that she wouldn't discuss it any more.'

Naomi fell silent, remembering. She and her mother had been content. How different life was after Jude arrived! Her mother had had no time for her any more, and things became worse when her baby brother was born. Naomi's eyes filled with tears as she thought of the long hours working in the bakery with no thanks from her stepfather. She winced as she remembered how he had often used his stick to hit her. Angrily, she brushed away her tears and forced herself to smile at her friend.

'Come on,' she said, swallowing hard and pointing to a small group of people sitting to one side of the path, 'let's see what's going on over there.'

In the centre of the group was a man, sitting at a small table and writing on a parchment. 'Then what did he say?' he asked, looking round at the group.

'Well,' someone replied, 'I remember he said we should love our enemies and pray for those who hurt us.' There was a pause while the man at the table scribbled furiously on his parchment. Another person in the crowd went on, 'Yes, and he also said that his Father makes the sun shine on evil people as well as on good people, and that we should forgive people who do bad things to us.'

'That's a hard teaching!' exclaimed a woman, and everyone nodded in agreement.

After a while, the man at the table stopped writing. 'I think that's enough for today,' he said. 'Thanks, everyone.' Then he gathered up his table and parchment and the group stood up to leave.

'Bye, Matthew,' they said to the man as they moved away. 'See you next week.'

'That man says he's going to write a book about Jesus one day,' Miriam said to Naomi, who was looking upset again.

'Well, I won't want to read it if it's full of all that rubbish,' Naomi replied crossly. 'Why should we love our enemies? How stupid is that?'

Chapter twenty-one

Naomi had passed through the gate Beautiful leading into the temple a few times since that day she had tried to steal money from the beggar who couldn't walk. Fortunately, she had gone at times when he wasn't there or when he was fast asleep. It was unlikely that he would recognize her now as before she had looked like a beggar herself, with her ragged clothes and dirty face. Now she was a healthy girl with clean clothes, very different from the thin child he had struck with his walking stick.

All the same, Naomi felt a little afraid when she and Miriam went into the temple courts one day. Today, the man was wide awake and was calling out for money from passers-by. How awful it would be if he did recognize her and told her friend how she had tried to steal from a lame man!

As they got closer, Naomi saw that many people were going past him and putting coins into his tin tray. Miriam began to reach into the pocket of her tunic to find a coin to give him, but as she did so the two men in front of them started talking to the beggar.

The beggar was looking up hopefully at the men, expecting them to give him money, but Naomi heard one of the men say to him, 'We don't have any silver or gold, but I'll give you what we do have.'

'It's Peter!' Miriam whispered. 'I wonder what he will give him!'

Then Peter spoke again: 'In the name of Jesus Christ, I order you to get up and walk!'

Miriam gripped her friend's arm so hard that it hurt. For in front of their eyes they saw Peter reach out his hand and help the lame man to his feet. A gasp came from the people nearby. They all knew this man. He had never been able to walk. Yet, as they watched, they saw him stand up! First he walked, but then he began to jump in the air, and pulling Peter and his friend John with him, he ran into the temple court, all the while shouting out his thanks to God!

As if in a dream, Naomi and Miriam joined the crowd who were following the dancing man. In the commotion, the man's tin tray was kicked over and a coin rolled towards Naomi as they passed. She glanced at Miriam to make sure she was looking the other way, then quickly bent down, picked up the coin and slipped it into her tunic pocket. It was only right that she should have it, she thought, although she wasn't sure why.

'Now you can't say you didn't see that, Naomi!' Miriam said breathlessly, turning to her friend. 'That was a miracle, wasn't it?'

Naomi nodded. 'It was amazing!' she said. 'I wonder how they did it!'

'You heard how they did it!' Miriam exclaimed. 'It was "In the name of Jesus!"'

'Maybe,' Naomi said, 'but Saul thinks Jesus is dangerous. Perhaps it was some kind of dark magic.'

'Oh Naomi!' her friend said in despair. 'How could someone who teaches love and forgiveness practise dark magic?'

'I don't know,' Naomi replied, 'but I'm suspicious.'

'Oh dear!' Miriam said. 'You sound just like Jacob!'

Naomi smiled. It pleased her to think she was like Jacob.

Chapter twenty-two

Naomi wasn't the only one who was suspicious. One day at lunch, Jeremiah reported that Saul had had a heated discussion in the temple with his teacher, Gamaliel. 'Saul seems to think Gamaliel is being too soft with the followers of Jesus,' Jeremiah told his wife.

'Why is that?' Hannah enquired.

'Well, apparently Gamaliel is advising the Jewish leaders to pay no attention to the followers of this new cult. He feels that if the talk about Jesus isn't true, then it will fizzle out. But if it turns out to be true, then they should be careful in case they find they have been fighting against God,' Jeremiah answered.

'That sounds sensible to me,' Hannah replied.

'Maybe,' her husband said, scratching his bald patch. 'Saul doesn't agree, though.'

Miriam said nothing. She had been told to keep her thoughts to herself, but she was convinced that what people were saying about Jesus was true. As for Naomi, she was just confused about it all. More and more people were following this 'Jesus movement'. They were calling themselves 'people of the Way'. Many healings were reported across Jerusalem. Jesus's disciples were preaching in the temple courts and in the synagogues, and hundreds were being baptised. There seemed to be no stopping them.

'What are you doing this afternoon, Miriam?' Naomi asked.

'I thought I'd go to the synagogue with Mother,' her friend answered. 'Do you want to come with us?'

'No thanks,' Naomi replied. She had been with them once or twice before and knew that they would go to the same synagogue where many of Jesus's followers went. 'I think I'll go for a walk down to the market.'

A little later, Naomi left the house and slowly made her way down the hill towards the city. She paused at a bend in the road to look across the valley at the hill beyond. From here she could see the splendid temple standing proudly above all the other buildings, the sunlight catching the gold on its roof and pinnacle. She was happy here in Jerusalem. Life was good. Hannah and Jeremiah cared for her as if she was one of their own children. Miriam was generous and kind. And Jacob … she smiled as she thought about him, so tall, brave and handsome! 'I wonder what he thinks of me?' she thought, smoothing her long dark hair as it fell around her shoulders.

Slowly, Naomi continued down the path, enjoying the gentle, cool breeze and the feeling of the sun on her face. She reached into the pocket of her tunic and felt the coin which she had kept hidden there. Her heart beat with excitement. Today she would spend it! Several days ago she had seen a beautiful bracelet in the market and she wanted it so much. It was made of silver and had a neat row of shiny red stones. And good fortune had come her way when the lame man's coin had rolled to her feet!

There seemed to be more people on the road today and some were gathering at the sides as if waiting for someone to come along. Naomi paused for a moment to watch a girl half carrying, half dragging a man to the side of the road, where the girl had already laid out a bed for him. She was about Naomi's age and was very thin and dirty. Without stopping to think, Naomi moved to the other side of the man to help support him as he staggered to the side of the road. He lay down with a sigh. 'Thank you, miss,' he said gruffly, and the girl looked up at her gratefully.

'Why do you want to sit him here in the hot sun?' Naomi asked the ragged girl. The man was obviously ill and should surely be resting in the cool of his home.

The girl's eyes shone. 'Peter will be walking down this road soon,' she explained. 'And when his shadow falls on my father, he will be made well again!'

Naomi shook her head. 'What rubbish!' she thought, and with a pitying smile she continued her walk towards the market.

But the excitement about buying the beautiful bracelet had gone. As she walked, Naomi could see in her mind the thin girl and her sick father. He was obviously unable to work and there were probably other children in the family who were hungry. Naomi thought of her own father and of how ill he had been just before he died. She remembered, too, what it felt like to be really hungry. She kicked a stone off the path in frustration and anger. The girl and her father had ruined her day!

Turning round, she retraced her steps until she came to the place where the girl and her father sat. With an impatient movement, she thrust her coin at the girl, who took it and held it in both hands, her eyes wide with gratitude and amazement.

But Naomi didn't stop to hear her thanks; she was too annoyed with herself and with the unfairness of her life. She wouldn't even be able to tell Hannah of her generosity, as the coin had been stolen in the first place.

Chapter twenty-three

Many new moons had come and gone since Naomi had given away her precious coin. She was now a little taller than when she had first arrived in Jerusalem and, as Hannah said, 'growing more beautiful every day'. Miriam, too, had grown a little, and her round face and shining eyes seemed to reflect a beauty that came from the inside. Naomi knew that her friend was happy in a way that she wasn't, and she blamed her mother and stepfather for this. She didn't want to think that it might be because of Jesus.

Despite what Gamaliel had said, the 'Jesus Way' hadn't fizzled out. It had continued to grow and was getting more organized, too. People were giving money to the leaders, and seven men had been chosen to share it out fairly among some of the Greek widows and others who were poor. And all over Jerusalem, groups of believers were meeting regularly to pray, study and remember Jesus.

At Saul's house, everyone was very careful not to talk about the Way. Sometimes, Hannah and Miriam would whisper quietly when they were working in the kitchen. But Jacob agreed with Saul that the Way had to be stopped, and Naomi was sure that they must be right. 'These disciples are claiming that Jesus was not just a

saviour for the Jews but for every nation in the world!'
Jacob explained. 'If we don't stop them, they'll take over
the synagogues and destroy our Jewish faith!'

Jeremiah, as usual, kept his opinions to himself.

'I hear that there's a trial of one of the Seven today,'
Jacob told them one day. 'His name is Stephen, he's a
Greek, and he seems to be causing a lot of trouble.'

He paused, and when Hannah raised an enquiring
eyebrow he continued: 'Yes, they say he's been arguing
with the Jewish leaders in his synagogue and saying that
Jesus was the Messiah! Some of them have even become
followers of the Jesus Way themselves.'

Miriam looked up at her brother and, speaking softly,
she commented, 'I can see that it's annoying for some of
the priests, but is it a crime to say Jesus is God's Promised
One?'

'That's enough, Miriam!' Jeremiah said sharply,
glancing over his shoulder to see if anyone else in the
household could hear.

Jacob cut in: 'Saul says Stephen's a heretic going round
telling lies. He's speaking against our holy temple and
blaspheming against God.'

Miriam bit her lip, and Hannah put her hand on her
arm to prevent her speaking again. Jeremiah smiled
kindly at her too, as if he understood, then he said, a little
reluctantly, 'Jacob and I have to go with Saul to the trial.'

'Do you want to go along too, girls?' Hannah asked. 'We
won't be allowed to go right into the court area, as that's
only for the men, but we'll be able to hear some of what's
going on from the women's court.'

Miriam nodded her agreement a little uncertainly while Naomi replied eagerly, 'Yes please, I've never been to a trial before!'

A large crowd had gathered by the time they reached the temple where Stephen was being tried. They walked together across the women's court and the men then went up the stone steps leading into the court where the trial was to be held. Naomi, Miriam and Hannah were not allowed any closer, so they settled themselves on a bench near the steps. There were large stone pillars between them and the area where the trial was to be heard, so they chose a place where they could see between them.

Saul, being an important person, was allowed to sit in a place close to the rows of benches set out for the men who formed the Sanhedrin. They were the Council, and it was their job to decide matters of religious law. Jeremiah and Jacob stood a little behind where Saul sat.

'Stephen will be allowed to defend himself in front of the Council,' Hannah reassured the girls. 'Gamaliel is the chief officer. He's a fair man and will make sure that everything is done correctly.'

They watched as the Sanhedrin entered and sat in their special seats, and Hannah leaned forward to see them more clearly. 'Oh dear,' she whispered to the girls, her hand going up to her necklace. 'That's the high priest, Caiaphas, in the centre seat. It means Gamaliel won't be in charge of the trial after all. He only does it when the high priest is away. That's not good.'

Chapter twenty-four

Hannah and Miriam waited anxiously as the man called Stephen was brought in front of the Council and the charges against him were read out. Naomi was sorry that they couldn't hear clearly what was going on, but at least they were able to see between the huge stone pillars that separated one court from another.

Stephen was standing up, so they were able to see him in the distance, and as they watched they were astonished to see that his face became like that of an angel—full of goodness and light! They held their breath for a moment and watched as he calmly turned to the Sanhedrin and began to speak.

Naomi and Miriam fidgeted on the bench. Stephen had been talking for a very long time and they could only catch the odd word here and there. 'He seems to be doing very well,' Hannah whispered. 'See how they're all listening to him. Perhaps the Council will see he has done nothing wrong.'

But at that moment, Stephen raised his voice and they listened in horror to his words that echoed clearly around the temple courts: 'You stubborn people! All down the ages the Jewish nation has refused to listen to the leaders God has sent to them. Now you have rejected and murdered God's most important messenger, Jesus!'

Suddenly, the mood in the court changed. The members of the Council were furious! They shook their fists and shouted angrily at Stephen. Hannah and the girls sat rigid on their bench, hardly daring to breathe. What was going to happen now?

Then Stephen spoke again. He was looking up as if he could see through the roof, and his face was alight with joy. 'Look,' he said, 'I can see Jesus in heaven itself, and he is standing at God's side!'

What happened next was very confusing and frightening. The trial hadn't finished, no witnesses had been called to speak, and no final judgement had been made. But the Council and most of the men in the court jumped up, covering their ears with their hands and yelling at the tops of their voices. They rushed at Stephen and began to drag him out of the temple. The violence of the men made Hannah and the girls tremble, and they shrank back as the mob rushed past, dragging Stephen with them.

Saul was part of the group, with Jeremiah and Jacob following behind. When Jacob saw the girls, he stopped and said, 'Did you hear his blasphemy? They're going to stone him to death! Are you coming with us?'

Hannah shook her head. 'No, dear, we're going back,' she said firmly. 'We've seen quite enough.'

'Oh, please let's go home quickly, Mother,' Miriam pleaded.

'What about you, Naomi? Do you want to come?' Jacob's brown eyes were sparkling and his face was red with excitement as he looked at her. 'You can come with me, but you'll have to be quick.'

Naomi flushed with pleasure. She wanted so much
to impress Jacob and make him realize how grown
up she was. Not that she particularly wanted to see
someone being stoned; she'd seen it before, of course,
as a punishment for people who broke the law. It was
unpleasant, but she didn't have to look. And she would be
with Jacob.

She turned eagerly to Hannah. 'Can I go with Jacob?'
she asked. 'Please?'

'Oh Naomi, I'd really rather you didn't,' Hannah
replied, but when she saw the girl's downcast face she
added rather sadly, 'Very well, if you must, but stay with
Jacob. And Jacob'—she turned to her son—'look after her
and keep away from trouble.'

Chapter twenty-five

Leaving Hannah and Miriam behind, Naomi followed Jacob, half walking, half running to keep up with him. By the time they caught up with the angry crowd, the prisoner had been taken out through the Beautiful gate of the temple and everyone was on their way towards the city walls. As they passed through the gate of the city, Naomi was dimly aware that this was the same gate through which she had entered Jerusalem when she came from Damascus. She looked up to the hill, almost expecting to see the man on the cross, just as she had seen him then.

People were picking up large stones now and hurling them at Stephen. Stephen was standing quite still and calm, which made Naomi feel suddenly very uneasy. He was guilty of blasphemy, she reminded herself, and should be killed. Some of the stones were badly thrown and missed their target, but quite a lot didn't, and Naomi could see that Stephen was getting hurt.

'Come on, Naomi, grab a stone,' Jacob urged, as he threw a large stone which hit Stephen on the shoulder.

Naomi bent and picked up a stone. She felt a bit sick and wished now that she had gone back with Hannah and Miriam. But she didn't want Jacob to think she was just a silly girl, so she got ready to throw her stone at Stephen. As she did so, she remembered all the pain and abuse she had suffered in the past, and a fierce anger washed over her. Suddenly, the man in front of her was everyone and everything that had ever hurt her—God, who had taken away her precious father; her mother, who had betrayed her; her stepfather, who was cruel and wicked. How she hated him!

With the roar of the crowd in her ears and the roar of anger in her heart, she lifted the stone. Fury put strength into her throw and the stone left her hand with a force that shocked her. It went spinning across the space between her and Stephen and struck him hard in the face.

'Well thrown!' Jacob cried with admiration. Naomi could see that Saul was standing to one side, nodding approvingly. But Naomi's anger had gone as quickly as it had come and she stood in the crowd now trembling and uncertain. Above the shouts and screams of the people she could hear Stephen praying, and every word stabbed at her heart: 'Lord Jesus, receive my spirit,' he said, and then he fell to his knees and cried out, 'Lord, don't hold this sin against them!' Then it seemed as if he fell asleep: he was dead.

The words from the man on the cross came to Naomi's mind: 'Father, forgive them, for they don't know what they're doing.' And here was Stephen, his follower, saying the same thing at more or less the same place. This time, however, the prayer seemed to be meant for her as well as others. For the first time in her life, Naomi felt dirty and bad. It wasn't a good feeling.

Chapter twenty-six

Jacob and Naomi were very quiet on their way home. Stephen's body had been taken by some of the disciples to be buried and the crowd had dispersed. Before they went, Saul had congratulated everyone and explained that these people of the Way had to be destroyed in order to protect God's name. Other followers of Jesus would need to be killed too, to make an example of those who turned away from the true faith.

'You OK, Naomi?' Jacob asked, looking down at her.

'I'm not sure,' Naomi replied miserably. 'What about you?'

'At the time,' Jacob replied, 'it was exciting. But now I wonder ...' His voice trailed off. Naomi nodded and no more was said until they reached home.

When they got back to the house, Jacob announced that he was going into the barn to see to the animals. Naomi went slowly into the house alone. Hannah looked up as she came in. She could see from Naomi's face that what she had dreaded had happened. 'So he's dead,' was all she said. Then seeing Naomi's eyes fill with tears, she opened her arms. 'Come here, child,' she said gently. Sobbing, Naomi ran to her and was gathered up against Hannah's chest.

'I threw a stone,' she said with a sob and felt Hannah stiffen. 'And it hit him. Why did I do that?'

Hannah said nothing but gently patted the girl's shaking shoulders. 'It's a bad business,' she said finally, 'and I'm afraid things could get a lot worse for those who are following Jesus.'

Hannah was right. Things did get worse. Over the next few days, Saul was a man with a single obsession. He was convinced that as a good Jew he ought to do all he could to oppose the name of Jesus. The chief priests gave him permission to punish Jesus's followers and to destroy the church of Jesus. Saul could be heard around the house making threats under his breath, and everyone in the household was uneasy. Every day, Saul would go from house to house and from synagogue to synagogue around Jerusalem and drag away men and women who followed the Way, beat them and put them in prison.

A few brave voices said that the stoning of Stephen had been illegal because he hadn't had a proper trial. Also, although the Jewish law allowed stoning for blasphemy, since the Romans had been in charge this was no longer permitted. Only a Roman court could sentence someone to death. But no one said any of this to Saul.

Followers of Jesus were leaving Jerusalem as fast as they could to avoid the persecution. They were travelling to other parts of Judea and Samaria for safety, but it seemed that wherever they went they talked about Jesus. So, instead of getting smaller, the number of Jesus's followers was actually growing at an alarming speed! Saul was furious.

Jeremiah had warned the family to keep any thoughts about Jesus to themselves. 'Saul says Jesus's followers are bad and are leading people astray,' he said to them. 'He says they must be stopped. It's important that we don't show any sympathy towards Jesus or Stephen, or we will be in danger ourselves.'

Suddenly, what had been a wonderful place for the family to live and work had become an unhappy place. Jeremiah and Hannah carried on with their work quietly and well, as they had always done, but their children could see that they were anxious. So when the family heard that Saul intended travelling with his household to Damascus to see if anyone in the synagogue there belonged to the Way, they received this news with mixed feelings.

'Saul has gone to Caiaphas, the high priest, this morning for letters to take to the synagogue leaders in Damascus, giving him permission to arrest anyone belonging to the Way,' Jeremiah confided to his wife. 'In some ways, this may be the answer to our problem. If we travel with him to Damascus, we can resign from our work once we get there. He can then return to Jerusalem without us.'

'We can't carry on like this,' Hannah agreed. 'It's a shame, though, as he's been a good employer and has treated us well.'

'Yes, but dragging people off to prison is not for me. I'm a peace-loving man,' her husband said sadly.

Naomi went very pale when she heard this conversation, and Miriam saw this immediately. 'But what about Naomi? She can't go back to Damascus, it's not safe!' she exclaimed.

'We can't leave her here either,' Jacob said. 'Look what happened when she was here alone before.'

'Naomi will stay with us,' Hannah said firmly. 'If she wants to live with us in Damascus, I'm sure her mother will allow it.'

'But will her stepfather?' Miriam asked anxiously.

'He won't have any choice,' Jacob said in a threatening voice which made Naomi feel a little better. 'We'll be there to make sure she's OK.'

Chapter twenty-seven

The journey back to Damascus couldn't have been more different from the journey Naomi had taken all those months before. Then, she had carried nothing but a bag with some food, a bottle of water, a blanket, a spare pair of shoes and her mother's purse. On this journey, they had no shortage of anything.

The only thing she had to carry now was a bottle of water and her mother's empty purse. Everything else was carried by the donkeys and camels: baskets full of barley bread, dried olives, figs and dates, an abundance of water, cooking pots, tents, plenty of bedding and spare clothes. Saul had the support of the high priest, and many officials from the temple had given him gifts to make his journey more comfortable. They had also sent him with temple officials and servants to make his task easier. He would need these provisions and extra men to escort the prisoners from Damascus back to Jerusalem.

Jeremiah and Hannah had made up their minds. Secretly, they felt that Saul had become a monster. They would not be returning to Jerusalem with him, but would stay in Damascus and look for work there. But their decision made Naomi very worried. When she had left Damascus, she had thought she would never go back; now the thought of seeing her mother, the baker's shop and her old home filled her with fear mixed with a kind of longing.

It was very hot and they had been travelling several hours, mostly in silence. The flat, empty landscape seemed to go on for ever, with just an occasional clump of cactus plants to break the continuous stretch of sand. Naomi sighed, and Hannah looked down at the girl walking beside her.

'How do you feel, Naomi—about going home?' Hannah asked.

'I don't know,' Naomi replied, her eyes downcast. 'I feel safe with you, but I also feel afraid and sad. I want to see Mother and my home again. But I don't want to live with her and that man. Yet I'm afraid she will want me to.'

Hannah nodded. She understood.

'But worst of all,' Naomi continued, looking up suddenly into Hannah's face, her eyes squinting in the sun, 'I feel bad.'

'Why is that?' Hannah asked softly, even though she thought she knew the answer.

'I threw a stone at a good man. He had done nothing to me.'

Naomi's eyes were full of tears. 'And that's not all I've done,' she went on. 'I'm a thief! I stole my mother's purse and the money she had saved up for food for the baby. And I stole food from the market stalls and money from beggars.'

Naomi searched Hannah's face to see if she was shocked, but her expression was gentle. She then looked down at her feet again and took a deep breath. 'I'm a liar too!' she continued. 'I lied to Miriam, who is my best friend, and told her I was with my aunt, instead of telling her the truth that I was running away. I lied to the shopkeeper about my age. And I said I didn't remember what happened when Miriam and I saw Jesus float up into heaven—but I did see him! And I didn't believe! I called Jesus a fool and his followers mad. I didn't even believe that the beggar had been healed because of Jesus, though I clearly heard what Peter said and saw the man walk with my own eyes! And can you believe it, Hannah? I enjoyed seeing Stephen suffer! I don't think anyone could forgive all that badness!'

'Hush, hush, child!' Hannah said, looking quickly round at the people walking near to them. 'Be careful!' She then leaned down to Naomi and dropped her voice to a whisper: 'I want to tell you some words I heard the disciple John say before we left Jerusalem. I think they will help you. He said that God loved the world so much that he gave his one and only Son. He said that God didn't send his Son into the world to judge people, but to save them! And anyone who believes in him will be forgiven!'

Naomi whispered back, 'Was John talking about Jesus?'

Hannah nodded, her fingers to her lips.

'What about you?' Naomi asked again. 'Do you think Jesus was God's Son?'

'I think he was,' Hannah said softly. 'And he came full of forgiveness for wicked people like you and me.'

'Oh no!' Naomi protested. 'You're not wicked! You're one of the best people in the world!'

Hannah laughed. 'I need to be forgiven just as much as you do, child!'

At that moment a voice interrupted them: 'What are you two discussing so seriously?' Jacob and Miriam had come to walk alongside them.

'Oh, this and that,' Hannah said vaguely.

'Father says we're going to set up camp here tonight,' Miriam told them. 'We've made good progress and we're almost halfway there.'

Chapter twenty-eight

There was plenty of time for thinking during the next few days. When the wind blew across the desert, anyone who talked risked getting a mouthful of dust. So for much of the journey they travelled in silence, the only sounds being the soft padding of the camels' feet over the rough, uneven ground and the rattling of the pans that hung from the donkeys' backs.

Naomi was glad she had confessed to Hannah. As she walked, she remembered all the things she had seen and heard about Jesus. She was sure now that he was the Jewish Messiah, the Promised One, but she knew she must keep her thoughts to herself. Saul was determined to destroy anyone who believed in Jesus, and Saul had many loyal supporters with him on this journey who felt the same as he did.

'Naomi, do you remember this caravan shelter?' Miriam cried out, dancing up beside her and interrupting her thoughts.

Naomi looked to see where Miriam was pointing and saw the shelter in the desert with the wayside inn and the well in the courtyard.

'Oh yes, I remember it!' Naomi exclaimed. 'It was where you discovered I was in the crowd travelling to Jerusalem!

I had tried to avoid you, as I was worried you'd guess I was running away!'

For the moment, their tiredness was forgotten as they ran to draw up the fresh, cool water from the deep well.

'We stop here for the Sabbath,' Jacob told the girls. 'The animals are ready for a day's rest.'

'And so are we!' Miriam said, laughing. 'Let's go and find a space upstairs for our mats, Naomi, before all the best places are taken!'

Once they had settled their belongings on the upper floor of the inn, the girls watched the adults unload the animals and settle them into their stalls on the lower floor. Hannah was taking out the barley bread, dates and figs from the baskets to give to the travellers once they had arranged their belongings.

'Do you need us, Mother?' Miriam asked.

'Not at the moment, dear,' Hannah replied, 'but don't wander too far!'

The two friends walked a little distance from the camp and stood together, staring out across the desert.

'It just seems to go on and on for ever,' Miriam remarked, and Naomi agreed. There was something rather wonderful about the sight of nothing: no hills or trees, houses or people—just the barren earth with only the odd rock or stubby cactus bush to break the emptiness. Standing there, Naomi and Miriam felt as if they were the only people in the universe.

'Miriam,' Naomi said impulsively, turning to her friend, who smiled encouragingly at her. 'Miriam, do you believe in Jesus?'

Miriam flushed a little before replying quietly, 'Yes, I do.'

'What do you believe?' her friend asked again, and Miriam replied in a rush, her words tumbling over one another, 'I believe he was the Messiah, and God's Son, that he did loads of miracles, that he died and came alive again, that he can forgive the bad things we've done, that he did float up into heaven (whatever you think), and that one day his followers will too!'

She stopped for breath and looked at Naomi, waiting for her to laugh. But Naomi didn't laugh.

'So do I,' Naomi said. 'I believe that too now. I'm sorry, Miriam, that I was so nasty about him, but I know now I was wrong.'

Miriam's bright eyes sparkled and her face lit up in a smile. 'I'm glad,' she said. 'I was sad when we didn't agree. Does that mean you feel happier now?'

Naomi thought for a moment. 'Yes, I suppose I do,' she said, a little surprised. 'And I don't feel as bitter and angry as I did—that's strange, isn't it?'

Chapter twenty-nine

It was difficult to speak freely when they were with the crowd of people. Everyone knew that to speak well of Jesus was dangerous, so they were careful not to mention his name. Hannah and Jeremiah were looking forward to getting away from Saul's employment.

They knew they were getting closer to Damascus when the rough, uneven track changed into the smooth Roman road. In the distance, they could see the mountains.

'Hopefully, we'll reach Damascus by nightfall,' Hannah told the two girls. 'It will be good to sleep on a proper bed!'

'I can't wait!' Miriam said in excitement, but Naomi bit her lip, and Hannah could see the fear and anxiety in her eyes.

After they had walked a little further, Hannah spoke again: 'Miriam, take these bottles of water to your father, please.' As Miriam took the water and ran ahead, Hannah turned to Naomi. 'Now we're alone, I want to ask you something,' she said.

Naomi looked up at Hannah, who continued, 'Naomi, can you find it in your heart to forgive your mother?'

Naomi didn't answer for several minutes. She remembered again the prayer she had heard in the temple: 'forgive us our sins, as we forgive those who sin against us'. When she had first heard those words, she had thought that the people were soft, but at this moment she agreed with the woman in Jerusalem who had said to Matthew that forgiveness was a hard teaching.

At last, Naomi answered, 'I know *he* has forgiven me'—not saying who 'he' was for fear of the listening ears around them—'so I suppose I must forgive her.'

She fell silent for a few minutes, but then asked, 'But why did she marry my stepfather? Do you know?'

Hannah smiled sadly. 'I don't suppose you realized that when your father died, your mother was told by his family that she had to marry his brother?'

Naomi looked up in surprise. 'No, she didn't tell me that!'

'I think you should know the truth,' Hannah continued. 'The problem was that, not only did your mother not want to remarry, but your stepfather didn't want to marry her either. He was going to marry a girl he had known for years, but because his brother died, he had to give up the girl he loved and marry your mother instead.'

'So that was why he was so bad-tempered,' Naomi said.

'Yes,' Hannah replied, 'and that was why he turned to drink.'

'He didn't have to take it out on me, though,' Naomi said bitterly.

'No, he didn't,' Hannah agreed. 'What he did to you was very bad, but he was an unhappy man.' She was about to say more, but at that moment Miriam and Jacob ran back to join them and their conversation ended.

'Not far now!' Jacob said. 'See how the countryside is changing!'

It was true. The brown desert was now occasionally splashed with green as more plants had pushed through the dusty soil. In the distance, the travellers could see the lush gardens lying around the ancient city kept so fertile by its two rivers which flowed all the year round.

'Oh,' sighed Miriam, 'I have missed the flowers and trees of Damascus!'

'Me too,' Jacob agreed, 'and especially the scrumptious apricots and pomegranates! The fruit in Jerusalem isn't as good as the fruit in Damascus.'

It was the middle of the day, the sun was very hot and the people were all looking forward to a wash, a good dinner and a comfortable night's sleep in the inn on Straight Street. Just a mile or so to go now.

Suddenly, there was a flash of bright light. Everyone stopped in their tracks. Even the donkeys and camels stopped dead. The light was so sudden and so blinding that Saul and his companions fell on the ground. Naomi noticed in amazement that the heavenly light made the midday sun seem quite pale.

'What's going on?' Miriam whispered fearfully. Before anyone could answer, they heard a voice which seemed to come from nowhere. They could hear the voice quite clearly, but couldn't understand what it was saying.

But Saul seemed to understand because he spoke to the voice: 'Who are you, Lord?' he asked. Again the voice spoke, but although everyone strained to hear, only Saul seemed to understand. The men around Saul were speechless. They could hear someone speaking but couldn't see who it was. Yet here was their leader, face down on the ground, looking terrified at what he was hearing.

No one moved for some time and then the voice stopped speaking. Saul raised his head and sat up. He rubbed his eyes with his hands and tried to get up. Jeremiah and a few other men reached out to help him to his feet, and as they did so, they realized that Saul couldn't see. The light had struck him blind!

Jeremiah and another man took hold of Saul's arms and together they led him along the last part of the journey towards the open gate into Damascus.

Chapter thirty

'Tell us what happened!' Miriam begged her father, as they sat together on the veranda of the Straight Street inn. The family had two rooms there, one for Jeremiah, Jacob and another of Saul's servants, and a smaller room for Miriam, Naomi and Hannah. Saul had been settled in his room with one of the temple priests as his 'eyes'. Jeremiah had been sad to see the great man made helpless and needing to be cared for like a baby.

The family had washed off the desert dust and had enjoyed a simple meal. They were glad to sit and rest their tired bodies. From their position on the veranda, they could see the familiar street they had walked down many times, the roof of their synagogue rising above the houses and the city wall in the distance.

Naomi felt very nervous about being back in her home town, but despite her fears, she too wanted to know what had happened to Saul as they entered Damascus. Jeremiah took a deep breath.

'Well,' he began, 'it all started with that incredible flash of light!'

'Yes, we all saw that,' said Hannah, 'and then we heard a voice, but it didn't make any sense.'

'Yet Saul seemed to understand it,' Jeremiah said, 'and he's sure that it was Jesus speaking!'

Jacob's mouth dropped open. 'What?' he spluttered. 'But that's impossible!'

'I know,' Jeremiah said. 'At first, Saul wasn't sure who it was. He said the voice asked him, "Saul, Saul, why do you persecute me?" That's why he then asked, "Who are you?" We didn't hear the answer, of course, but Saul did, and he says that the voice said, "I am Jesus whom you are persecuting!"'

'What happened then?' Naomi asked, her eyes now wide with excitement.

'Well, that's what's so strange. Apparently, Saul was told to get up and go into the city, where he would be told what to do next.'

'Could it have been a dream, or perhaps a fit, do you think?' Jacob asked. 'I've heard of people seeing and hearing things when they've been in the sun for too long.'

Jeremiah shrugged his shoulders. 'I've no idea,' he said. 'Saul is certain it was Jesus speaking to him, and he's now full of remorse about persecuting Jesus' followers.'

Naomi leaned back in her chair and stared out into the Damascus street. She knew now that it was true. Jesus was alive and he had somehow appeared to Saul. She shut her eyes and thought back over the chat she had had with Hannah earlier in the day. Could she find it in her heart to forgive her mother? 'Yes,' she thought, 'I can forgive her. I know she is sorry and must miss me as much as I miss her.' At that moment, she wished more than anything else in the world that she could run from the inn down the road and into her home. 'But I could never forgive him,' she thought. 'He's not even sorry for what he did to me.

And because of him, I must keep away from my mother for ever.'

With a sigh, she opened her eyes. It was beginning to get dark, and apart from a man with a donkey delivering bread there was no one in the street. She watched the donkey slowly plodding towards them, remembering how this had been her job when she lived with her mother. The man looked tired; no doubt he was at the end of his round and would soon pack up for the day. She idly watched as the man turned his donkey towards the entrance of the inn, and in that moment she recognized him. With a gasp of horror, she jumped off her chair and hid, cowering behind the cactus hedge that framed the veranda.

Hannah and Jeremiah had recognized Jude at the same moment as Naomi and sat very still, watching as he went into the kitchen. After a few minutes he came out again, having unloaded the donkey of its baskets of bread. He was intent on leading the donkey round the path and out again onto the road, so he didn't look up to see the family who were silently watching him.

'It's OK, Naomi, he's gone,' Jacob said kindly, his strong arms helping her to her feet and sitting her gently in her chair again. Her face was as white as a sheet and she was trembling with the shock of seeing her stepfather. Miriam took her shaking hands and held them tight. 'We'll look after you, Naomi. We won't let that evil man hurt you, will we, Father?'

'Hush, Miriam,' he scolded. 'I don't believe he's evil, but no, we won't let him hurt Naomi.'

Hannah put her arm around Naomi. 'You'll be safe with us, Naomi,' she said. 'Besides, no one knows we're here in Damascus.'

Chapter thirty-one

'What are we going to do, Mother? We've been here nearly three days. We can't stay in this inn for ever.'

Hannah turned to look down at her daughter. 'We have to wait, dear,' she said quietly. 'At the moment, Saul needs your father to help him to get around. Once we know what will happen to him, we can think about our own plans.'

Miriam sighed. 'Have you managed to get Saul to eat yet?'

'No, I haven't,' Hannah answered. 'He's determined that he won't have any food until someone called Ananias comes to visit him.'

'Does he know this Ananias?' Miriam asked.

'No, that's the strange thing,' Hannah replied. 'Saul says that God told him in a vision that this man would heal him of his blindness.'

Naomi, who was listening to this conversation, said, 'Jacob says he's praying day and night and is refusing to eat or drink anything. He'll die if he carries on like this.'

'Shall we take him some fresh apricots, Mother?' Miriam said. 'Naomi and I picked these from the garden this morning and they're really juicy and sweet.'

'You can if you like, girls, but I don't think you'll succeed,' Hannah said wearily.

As the two girls got near to Saul's room, they saw a man they didn't recognize in the doorway, being invited in. Full of curiosity, they moved closer, the basket of apricots in their hands. As they stood hesitating at the open door, wondering if they should go in, they heard to their amazement the man introducing himself as Ananias!

Naomi felt Miriam grasp her arm tightly. Together, they held their breath and watched as Saul quickly stood up to greet the man. Then Ananias put his hands on Saul and said, 'Brother Saul, the Lord Jesus, who appeared to you on the road as you were coming here, has sent me so that you may see again and be filled with the Holy Spirit.' At that moment, the girls saw something fall out of Saul's eyes, something scaly like pieces of dry skin, and it was quite clear to them that he could see again!

All was confusion for a while. Everyone was talking at once, and the girls couldn't understand what was going on. Ananias said something about Saul being baptized, and Saul immediately agreed, his face alight with a happiness they had never seen there before. Some of Saul's men didn't seem very pleased about this idea, but they were ignored. Then the girls saw Saul and Ananias, with Jeremiah, Jacob and a few others, moving towards the door. Quickly, they stepped out of the way.

The group of men came out of the room, passing the two girls standing in the passage. Jeremiah paused and came over to them. 'Saul is going with Ananias to the river. He's going to be baptized!' he whispered to them. 'He's a changed man! He's a follower of Jesus now, just as we are! It's wonderful! Tell Mother to prepare a meal. When he returns, he'll be very hungry!'

Then he quickly followed the group out of the inn and down the street.

For a few minutes, the girls remained motionless, as if unable to believe their eyes and ears. Then, still holding the basket of apricots, they ran back to Hannah to report what they had seen.

Chapter thirty-two

How different everything was now! Since Saul had become a follower of the Way, they were able to talk about Jesus freely and without fear. It was true, of course, that some of the temple officers who had come with Saul to arrest the followers of Jesus weren't very happy about Saul's change of heart, but no one seemed too worried about them. They had disappeared off to the synagogue to report the change of plan and didn't return to the inn.

Everyone agreed that Ananias was a very brave man. The news had already reached the followers of Jesus that Saul had come to Damascus to arrest them, so Ananias had taken a risk in going to meet him. But it seemed that God had spoken very clearly to him and told him to go to Saul, so that is what he had done.

'This afternoon, Saul is going to the home of one of the believers in Jesus,' Jeremiah told the family when they met for lunch. 'The followers of the Way are gathering so that they can hear his story,' he continued. 'We're all invited too.'

Hannah beamed. 'It will be wonderful to be able to talk about Jesus and sing songs together without being afraid,' she said.

Naomi hadn't yet stepped foot outside the inn since arriving in Damascus, for fear of bumping into her stepfather. 'I'd like to go,' she said, 'but is it safe?'

'You must come,' Miriam insisted. 'We'll all be with you, and Jacob will keep close to you.'

Jacob's deep brown eyes smiled down at her. 'You'll be fine, Naomi,' he said.

So it was that after they had had an afternoon rest, they all gathered at the entrance of the inn and set out together to the home where the meeting was to be held. It seemed strange to Naomi to be walking down Straight Street again. So much had happened to her since the time she had run down this road towards the city gate. Yet everything looked exactly the same as it had done then. The fig tree on the corner of the weaver's house was still there, as was the broken gate that led up to the butcher's shop. She jumped in alarm as a donkey laden with baskets suddenly rounded the corner, but it was carrying oranges, so she relaxed again.

Naomi looked around anxiously when she saw the checkpoint and the Roman soldier sitting dozing in the sun, just as he had done the day she ran away. They were getting too close to her family home. Jacob noticed that she was worried and quickly put his arm round her shoulders, while she lowered her head to hide her face from anyone who might look out of the window of her house. Soon they would be past the house and she would be able to breathe freely again.

'Goodness!' Hannah suddenly exclaimed, and Jeremiah said, 'Oh dear, should we go back?'

Naomi jerked up her head and saw with horror that they were walking up the path to her house! But it was too late to turn back. At the door welcoming Saul and Ananias into the home was her mother, holding a small child in her arms. A little boy stood beside her, holding the hand of a man. That man was Jude, her stepfather. Naomi stopped dead. One part of her wanted to turn and run away, but the other wanted to throw her arms around her mother. The group hadn't seen her yet, so she had a few moments of indecision.

Feeling desperate, she looked up at Jacob, who was looking at the couple in the doorway with his mouth open. Then he pulled himself together. 'Naomi,' he said in a firm voice, 'I think this is a good time for you to let your mother see you.'

Naomi nodded miserably, and with Jacob on one side and Hannah on the other, she moved forward towards her mother.

The cry that came from her mother made everyone stop in their tracks. She thrust the child into Jude's arms and ran the few steps towards Naomi, sobbing as she flung her arms around her.

'My daughter!' she cried, the tears pouring down her face. 'My own daughter, Naomi! Oh, how I have longed to see you!'

Naomi couldn't speak, for she was crying too. She simply clung on to her mother as if she would never let her go.

Chapter thirty-three

Everyone else had gone into the house where the believers were meeting, leaving Rebecca and Naomi outside.

'Let me look at you,' Rebecca said, pushing Naomi slightly away from her so that she could see her face properly. 'You're looking very well,' she added sadly. 'I can see that Hannah and Jeremiah have taken good care of you. I'm so grateful to them.'

Naomi looked up into her mother's face. It didn't look as white and strained as it had done before and, despite her sadness, there was something in her eyes that hadn't been there since the day her father died.

'Hannah and Jeremiah say that I can live with them for always, Mother,' Naomi said quickly, 'and I think it would be best. I can't live in the same house as that man. You do understand, don't you?'

'Yes, of course I understand,' her mother said. 'We don't deserve for you to even want to come to visit us. I'm so sorry I didn't protect you from his tempers. I was weak and stupid. Can you forgive me?'

Naomi nodded, her eyes full of tears. 'I can. You see, Jesus has forgiven me, and he said that we have to forgive others if we want to feel his forgiveness.'

At this, her mother burst into noisy tears again. Naomi, alarmed, said, 'What's the matter, Mother? Why are you crying?'

After a while, Rebecca pulled herself together and, half laughing and half crying, said, 'I'm crying because I'm happy! You see, things have changed for us too. Jude came back from Jerusalem a different man! He says that when he heard Peter speaking at Pentecost, he realized what a bad man he had been. He asked Peter what he should do, and Peter told him to believe on the Lord Jesus and he would be saved. And he did believe! And he was saved! And now I am saved too! And you are too! And I'm so happy!'

Naomi was stunned. She was happy that her mother was a follower of the Way, but she couldn't believe what she was hearing about her stepfather. She hadn't thought that she would ever have to talk to him again or even think about him. But now she might have to forgive him too. That was too much to expect of her.

From the inside of the house came the sound of singing. 'Saul has obviously told his story,' Naomi said. 'I'm sorry you didn't hear it, Mother—it's amazing!'

Rebecca smiled. 'You can tell me all about it in good time,' she said. 'You will visit regularly, won't you, when you're with Hannah and the family? There's no need to be afraid of Jude any more—he's a much nicer person now that he's stopped drinking.'

Naomi nodded but didn't answer.

'Shall we go inside?' Rebecca suggested. Naomi agreed, so together, hand-in-hand, the two walked up the stone steps and into the house that Naomi had run away from.

It looked much cleaner than it used to, and the cooking pots had been polished so that they were shining brightly on the kitchen shelf. Where there had been blackened walls, Jude had painted them with whitewash so that they were white and clean.

As they entered the main room, the singing stopped and the people began to say 'The Lord's prayer' together. Naomi was surprised to see that Jude seemed to be leading the prayer and the people were following him. 'Our Father in heaven …' Naomi smiled to herself as she remembered how annoyed she had been when she first heard this prayer. She moved closer to her friend Miriam, who looked anxiously at her before continuing with the words, 'and forgive us our sins, as we forgive those who sin against us'.

Naomi didn't join in saying the prayer with the others. 'I'm not sure I can forgive *him* that easily,' she thought to herself. 'I could have died, and it would have been his fault.'

Chapter thirty-four

'Have you spoken to him yet, Naomi?' Miriam asked her friend. 'Your stepfather, I mean?'

Several days had passed since that emotional reunion with her mother. The group had moved out of the inn and were now living in a house just off Straight Street, not far from Naomi's family. Saul was staying with one of the believers who lived near the synagogue. This was more convenient for him, because he went to the synagogue every day to speak to the Jewish people. He was trying to persuade them that Jesus was the Messiah promised by Daniel and other prophets who had lived hundreds of years before.

The two girls had done their jobs for Hannah and were walking towards Naomi's old home to collect some bread when Miriam had suddenly asked her the question.

'No,' Naomi answered, 'I haven't spoken to him. He's usually at the synagogue when I go home, so I'm managing to avoid him.'

'You won't be able to avoid him for ever, though, will you?' Miriam said, tucking her black curls behind her ears.

'I know,' Naomi said. There was a pause. Then, when Miriam could see that Naomi wasn't going to say anything else, she asked again, 'Do you think you'll ever be able to forgive him?'

Naomi looked at her friend rather sadly. 'I do try to forgive him,' she said, 'but every time I try, I remember the horrid things he said, the way he shouted at me and how he hit me when he was drunk.'

Miriam nodded. 'I think I'd find it impossible to forgive him too,' she said, sympathizing.

They had now arrived at Naomi's home, and as they ran inside, Naomi's brother gave a shriek of excitement and ran towards them. He looked forward to Naomi's visit each day as he knew that she was always ready to play a game with him. Already Naomi loved him and her little sister very much.

Rebecca was giving the little girl a bath and was glad to get some help. As Naomi watched, her mother said, 'She looks just like you did at that age!' Naomi smiled to think that she was once so small and helpless.

After an hour or so, Miriam said they needed to return home with the bread, so Naomi gave her mother, brother and sister a hug, picked up the basket of bread and promised to come again the next day. As the girls passed the kitchen, Naomi saw a big batch of bread dough on the warm shelf, left there to rise before being baked. She felt very sad to realize that, as well as looking after the children, her mother had to make the loaves for her husband to sell at the market.

'Are you coming, Naomi?' Miriam said impatiently, as her friend stood hesitating at the door.

'Of course,' Naomi replied, and the two left the house.

On their way home, they heard the sound of loud voices as they walked past the turning which led to the synagogue.

'I wonder what's going on,' Miriam said with surprise. 'Let's go and see.'

As they entered the building, the voices grew louder, and they heard that the people were talking about Saul.

'How dare he say Jesus is the Son of God!' one of the men shouted. 'That's blasphemy!'

'First he causes havoc in Jerusalem, arresting the followers of this man, and now he's saying he's the only way to be saved!' said another.

'I'm not so sure he's wrong,' came a voice from the crowd, 'What if Jesus really is the Messiah?'

'Of course he's not!' shouted back the first man. 'Jesus is dead, isn't he?'

'But Saul says he came alive again!'

The arguments went backwards and forwards.

'I think we should leave,' Naomi whispered. Miriam agreed, and they walked the rest of the way home in silence. This disturbance reminded them of the uproar in the temple when Stephen was in front of the court. It was an uncomfortable thought.

Chapter thirty-five

'**D**o you think we have to forgive people even if they don't say sorry?' Naomi asked Hannah several days later.

Hannah looked down at Naomi's serious face. 'Well, I think we should ask God to help us to do that, yes,' she answered. 'I'm not saying it would be easy, though, and I certainly don't think we can do it on our own.'

Naomi knew she was right. She thought back to the day she had seen Jesus on the cross, and how the people had been shouting insults at him and spitting on him. She could still hear his words: 'Father forgive them, for they don't know what they're doing.' She also remembered with shame the day she had thrown a stone at Stephen, and how he had said, 'Lord, don't hold this sin against them' just before he died.

It was afternoon, the time of day Naomi liked the best. Most mornings now she went to help her mother with the children and with baking the bread for the afternoon delivery. She still hadn't spoken to her stepfather, and if he ever came to the house, she would make an excuse and leave as soon as possible. The afternoons were generally spent sitting on the veranda drinking grape juice and chatting to Hannah and Miriam.

Miriam wasn't listening to Naomi's conversation with Hannah. She was thinking about the events of the past few days. The believers in Jesus had grown to a huge number. They were now meeting in a different home, as Rebecca and Jude's house wasn't big enough. There seemed to be rumours going around that some of the synagogue members were planning ways to stop Saul spreading the message. But Saul just carried on preaching.

Suddenly, Jacob and Jeremiah appeared on the veranda breathing heavily, as if they had been hurrying. There was another man with them, and Naomi shrank back when she saw that it was her stepfather. She looked around to see where she could escape to, but the men were standing between her and the door to the house. Then she saw that the men were too worried to notice her, so she sat very still as Hannah asked quickly, 'What is it?'

'It's Saul,' Jacob answered. 'He's discovered there's a plot to kill him.'

'Is it true, Jeremiah?' Hannah asked her husband, her hands going up to the beads around her neck.

'It appears so,' Jeremiah answered slowly.

'Then he must leave Damascus!' Hannah cried. 'It's not safe for him here!'

Jude spoke up: 'We agree he needs to leave. But the trouble is that Saul's enemies are watching the city gate day and night. If he attempts to just walk out, they will kill him!'

'We need to think of a way to get him out,' Miriam said, leaning forward. 'Naomi managed to escape without being seen—perhaps she can help.'

Naomi flushed as the men turned towards her. She saw that her stepfather was looking at her as if waiting for her to answer, but, before she could open her mouth, he cleared his throat: 'I think I need to say something to you all,' he said, and Naomi noticed with surprise that the harsh voice she had been so afraid of had gone.

'I need to ask you all to forgive me,' Jude went on. 'I was very rude to you all when I visited you in Jerusalem. I want to say how grateful I am for the way you cared for my daughter.'

Hannah smiled. 'We have loved having her as part of our family,' she said.

'But most of all,' Jude continued, 'I have to say sorry to Naomi.' He turned to her. 'I treated you very badly. No child should be shouted at and beaten as I did to you. I don't expect you to forgive me, but all I can say is that everything has changed since I trusted in Jesus. I hope that, maybe in time, we can be friends,' he finished humbly.

Naomi didn't know what to say. There was a silence as everyone seemed to be waiting for her to reply. Jacob could see she was struggling within herself. 'I think Naomi needs a bit of time to think about that,' he said kindly to Jude, 'but thanks for saying it.'

Naomi looked up at Jacob, her eyes full of gratitude.

'Now,' Jacob continued, 'how are we going to get Saul out of Damascus?'

'Yes,' Miriam said. 'How did you get out, Naomi? Did you hide in a cart or something?'

Naomi shook her head. 'No, I just walked out with everyone else. That won't work for Saul.' She paused. 'But,' she continued, her eyes sparkling, 'I've got an idea!'

She explained how she had thought about going through the hole in the city wall, but had decided she couldn't do that because of the long drop to the ground below. 'The hole I found is big enough. If we hid him in one of your bread baskets,' she turned to Jude, 'and attached some rope to the handle, we could lower him down that way.'

Chapter thirty-six

Everyone agreed this was a splendid plan. In order not to attract attention, only Jacob and Jude went with Naomi to see the hole in the city wall that she had found such a long time before. Then a message was sent to Saul that he should get ready. The friends who would be travelling with him were told to leave during the day through the gate and then hide somewhere outside the city wall to wait for Saul to be lowered down.

The plan was that they would all meet at the city wall after it had got dark. Jude went home to find a bread basket large enough to fit a person inside. Jacob was sent off to the rope-maker's to buy some very strong rope. 'I can't tell them what I want it for,' he thought to himself, 'so I'll say it's got to be strong enough to pull a cart.' Jeremiah went round to find some strong young men who could help. 'You'll need several people to keep hold of the rope as we lower it down,' he was told. And Hannah and Rebecca packed up food and water to send with the party, while Miriam and Naomi looked after the children.

At last it was time. It was a particularly dark night when Hannah, Jeremiah, Jacob and the two girls left the house and made their way up Straight Street.

'We can start off using a lantern,' Jeremiah said. 'If anyone asks, we're going to visit friends.'

Their hearts were beating fast as they made their way through the city.

The Roman guard was, for once, awake. He had been warned to keep an eye open for Saul and to stop him leaving the city. But he took no notice of them. At one point, they passed a couple of the leaders of the synagogue, who peered suspiciously at them out of the darkness. But when they saw it was a family and that they had turned in the opposite direction from the gate, they lost interest.

They were getting closer to the city wall now. Jeremiah put out their lantern and together they moved silently in the darkness towards their meeting place. Naomi led the way, as she knew it well. Many times she had stood looking through this gap in the wall, wondering how she could escape through it; now she would see how it could be done!

As they arrived, Naomi could see the shadows of several men standing there. Miriam clutched at Naomi's hand. She wasn't sure if she was afraid or excited. It was probably both. No one said a word. Saul was already inside the basket, with just his head and shoulders showing. If it hadn't been so serious, it would have been funny to see this great man in a basket. Nobody was laughing, though. Everyone knew that if they were discovered by those wanting to kill Saul, there would be no escape.

With great care, Jude and three other men lifted the basket into the hole in the wall, while Jeremiah, Jacob and two others held tightly onto the rope. Hannah and the two girls stood silently, holding their breath, Hannah clasping both her hands together as if in prayer. If they let go of the basket, Saul would almost certainly fall to his death.

Slowly, slowly, the basket was eased through the gap. There was a frightening moment when it tipped over the other side and swung perilously to and fro as the men held tightly onto the rope. With great care, they managed to lower the basket to the ground on the other side of the wall. Naomi watched as the men gradually let out the rope which on their side got shorter and shorter. Would there be enough rope to get Saul safely to the ground?

Then, with a little jerk, the rope slackened. Jude whispered, 'He's landed!' and they were able to let go. Of course, everyone wanted to look quickly through the hole in the wall to see the small party down below who were there to help Saul as he climbed out. With a quick wave, they turned and disappeared into the darkness. The empty basket was quickly pulled up and the believers turned to hug one another as they said goodbye.

Jude leaned down to Naomi. 'Thank you, Naomi,' he said. 'That was a wonderful plan, and with God's help we have succeeded.' And in the darkness, Naomi smiled at him and put her hand in his. 'Yes,' she whispered back, 'we did it together.'

Also available

DISCOVERING THE HIDDEN LAMB

Gill Jacobs

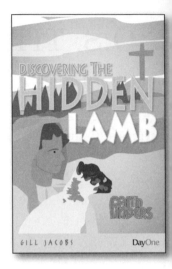

A story of two lambs: the orphaned lamb Ben cares for, and Jesus, the Lamb of God. Bible events woven into this story are seen through Ben's eyes as he struggles to understand who Jesus is while trying to save his pet lamb from being sold for sacrifice at Passover. The reader discovers what life was like in Palestine during Jesus' time, and why the Lamb of God had to die.

Much of Gill Jacobs' working life has been with young people both within the church and as a Paediatric Occupational Therapist. She runs training in special needs for professionals and has also been involved in writing parenting courses. Her husband John is a Messianic Jew. They live in Hampshire and have two grown-up daughters.

Also available

S.O.S. TITANIC

Jill Silverthorne

Chrissie and Luke Barwell are surprised to find themselves invited on a trip to America by an aunt they scarcely know. Their journey promises more than they expect when they secure a passage on the White Star Line's newest ocean-going liner. Chrissie, though, is uncertain from the beginning about what the trip may hold.

Based on events of April 1912, the journey turns out to be much more significant than any of the travellers could imagine. How will they cope with the life and death situations they face?

Jill Silverthorne was born and bred in South Wales and it was there she committed her life to Christ. She graduated from the University of Leicester with a degree in English and went on to teach at a sixth form college, before leading a faculty and then becoming deputy headteacher in a secondary school in the Midlands. Jill has always loved working with young people in her job and in church settings. She enjoys preparing youth-based resources for holiday clubs, camps and church youth groups. She has been published in association with her work and also worked with several Christian organisations, writing resources for ministries to teenagers. Jill has a passion to see high quality Christian literature written for young people in the twenty first century. This is her first contribution towards seeing that aim fulfilled.

Also available

THE SECRET OF THE HIDDEN TUNNEL

Mary Weeks Millard

Matty Morris's world collapses when her parents announce that they are going to move to Africa and that she will need to go to boarding school. She is sure she won't like St Anne's, but she quickly settles in and makes friends. Through a series of adventures and personal challenges she and her friends make exciting discoveries about the school's history as well as some life-changing decisions ...

Mary Weeks Millard used to work as a missionary in Africa. She now loves to write stories for younger readers.

Also available

THE MYSTERY OF THE DESERTED HOUSE

Mary Weeks Millard

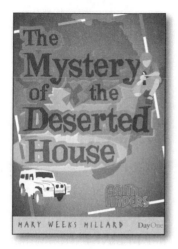

Spike, Joe and Matt are playing their usual ballgame when they find the deserted house. The gate is rusty, the grass is overgrown, there is a half-built extension, and an old Land Rover is abandoned in the garden. The boys are intrigued and, over time, start to explore the rooms inside. But the more time they spend there, the more mysterious they find it, and their exploration of the house eventually leads them into danger. What is the secret of this mystery house, and why did its owners leave it like this?

Mary Weeks Millard used to work as a missionary in Africa. She now loves to write stories for younger readers.

Also available

NEVER GIVE UP ON YOUR DREAMS

Mary Weeks Millard

Gabrielle is six years old when her swimming instructor realizes that she has a natural talent and arranges for her to have extra swimming coaching. Through her dedication and self-discipline, and with the support of her family and especially her granny, Gabrielle gets better and better, and everyone thinks that she will soon be able to compete in the Olympics. She dreams of winning an Olympic gold. But one day, disaster strikes. What will happen to her Olympic dreams now?

Mary Weeks Millard used to work as a missionary in Africa. She now loves to write stories for younger readers.

Also available

RICHES IN ROMANIA

Rebecca Parkinson

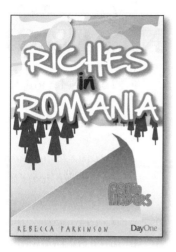

Jenny's parents have always been able to give her everything she wants until her dad begins a new job working for a Christian charity. As Jenny struggles to come to terms with their new lifestyle, her family is invited to take part in a farming project in Romania and Jenny sets off on an adventure that will ultimately change her life! As Jenny and her brother David spend time in a small Romanian village they make friends with the local children and begin to realise that friendship can break down barriers of wealth, language and culture. However when Jenny's precious locket goes missing it seems that everything has gone wrong, until a guard, previously in the Communist regime, teaches her the secret of forgiveness and encourages her to set about putting things right in her own life.

Rebecca Parkinson lives in Lancashire with her husband, Ted, and their two children. A teacher and leader of the youth work in her church, she loves to spend her free time writing stories for children. Rebecca has enjoyed visiting family and friends living in different parts of the world, where she has met many inspirational people. It is these visits that have inspired this book.

About Day One:

Day One's threefold commitment:

~ To be faithful to the Bible, God's inerrant, infallible Word;

~ To be relevant to our modern generation;

~ To be excellent in our publication standards.

I continue to be thankful for the publications of Day One. They are biblical; they have sound theology; and they are relative to the issues at hand. The material is condensed and manageable while, at the same time, being complete—a challenging balance to find. We are happy in our ministry to make use of these excellent publications.
JOHN MACARTHUR, PASTOR-TEACHER,
GRACE COMMUNITY CHURCH, CALIFORNIA

It is a great encouragement to see Day One making such excellent progress. Their publications are always biblical, accessible and attractively produced, with no compromise on quality. Long may their progress continue and increase!
JOHN BLANCHARD, AUTHOR, EVANGELIST AND APOLOGIST

Visit our web site for more information and to request a free catalogue of our books.

In the UK: www.dayone.co.uk

In North America: www.dayonebookstore.com